10/13

KENT LIBRARIES
WITHDRAWN STOCK

Books should be returned or renewed by the last date
above. Renew by phone **08458 247 200** or online
www.kent.gov.uk/libs

Libraries & Archives

C333424375

Don't You Know There's a War On?

Don't You Know There's a War On?

WORDS AND PHRASES FROM THE WORLD WARS

Nigel Rees

BATSFORD

First published in the United Kingdom in 2011 by

Batsford
Old West London Magistrates' Court
10 Southcombe Street
London W14 0RA

An imprint of Anova Books Company Ltd

Copyright © Batsford 2011
Text © Nigel Rees 2011

ISBN: 978 1 906388 99 7

A CIP catalogue record for this book is available from the British Library.

18 17 16 15 14 13 12 11
10 9 8 7 6 5 4 3 2 1

Reproduction by Mission Productions, Hong Kong
Printed by Everbest Printing Co., Ltd in China

This book can be ordered direct from the publisher at the website
www.anovabooks.co.uk, or try your local bookshop.

Distributed in the United States and Canada by
Sterling Publishing Co., 387 Park Avenue South,
New York, NY 10016, USA

INTRODUCTION

The naming of wars is an odd business. It usually depends which side you are on, of course. I believe that the Boers referred to what we know as 'the Boer Wars' as *Vryheidsoorloeë* (literally, 'freedom wars'). The Vietnamese called the Vietnam War 'the American War', understandably enough.

Sometimes the war does not have to be over before the name is applied. The Gulf War was being called by that name in January 1991 and the war was not wrapped up until March of that year.

And then there is the question of when a war is not a war. I still note a general hesitation in referring to 'the Falklands conflict' of 1982 as a war. So where does that leave the late unpleasantness, not really over yet, in Iraq? 'The Iraq War' may be winning the day. 'The Iraqi Regime Change'? 'The American Invasion of Iraq'? Only time will tell.

Looking back to the world wars that are the source of this book's words and phrases, it is remarkable to discover just how soon both of them came to be given their grandiloquent but ominous titles. The term 'world war' is defined by the *OED*, a touch loosely you might think, as a 'war involving many important nations'. It was first recorded in 1909. Five years later there came the real thing.

Initially, of course, **the First World War** was not known as this. It was being called **the European War** as early as 14 September 1914, a mere few weeks into the fray. On that day, the *Lima Daily News* in Ohio was offering 'Latest European War Map Given by the News to every reader presenting this coupon and 10 cents ... '

A book of poems by H.D. Rawnsley was given the title *The European War 1914–15* as early as 1915. It is, however, a satisfactorily accurate name because, although nations strictly speaking beyond Europe, like Turkey, were involved, and in due course Australia, New Zealand and, above all, the United States joined in, the cause and focus of the war were very much European.

The term 'European War' was still being invoked in the 1920s – as the phrase's use on numerous war memorials attests. To this day, the London Library categorizes books like Winston Churchill's *The World Crisis* under the heading 'H[istory]. European War I' and his *The Second World War* under 'H. European War II'.

Almost as rapidly, the conflict became chiefly known as **the Great War** – and why not? In terms of scale and mortality there had certainly never been anything like it before. As early as October 1914, *Maclean's Magazine* (in the US) was stating, 'Some wars name themselves … This is the Great War'. Previously, the name had been given to the French Revolutionary and Napoleonic wars of 1793–1815. As Arnold Toynbee pointed out, the British kept on using this name until the fall of France in 1940 'in order to avoid admitting to themselves that they were now again engaged in a war of the same magnitude.'

By 10 September 1918 – i.e. just before the Armistice was signed – Lieut. Col. C. à Court Repington was referring to it in his diary as the 'First World War', thus: 'I saw Major Johnstone, the Harvard Professor who is here to lay the bases of an American History. We discussed the right name of the war. I said that we called it now *The War*, but that this could not last. The Napoleonic War was *The Great War*. To call it *The German War* was too much flattery for the Boche. I suggested *The World War* as a shade better title, and finally we mutually agreed to call it *The First World War* in order to prevent the millennium folk from forgetting that the history of the world was the history of war.' Repington's book entitled *The First World War 1914–18* was published in 1920. Presumably this helped popularize the name for the war, while ominously suggesting that it was the first of a series.

There is rather more to the naming of **the Second World War** than that. After the First World War, what could be more natural than to have the Second World War? But, of course, it was not immediately recognized as such. At first, some tried to refer to it, once again, as 'the war in Europe', but *Time* Magazine was quick off the mark in 1939: 'World War II began last week at 5:20am (Polish time) Friday, September 1, when a German bombing plane dropped a projectile on Puck, fishing village and air base in the armpit of the Hel Peninsula ... '

Soon after this, Duff Cooper published a book of his collected newspaper articles entitled *The Second World War*. When it quite clearly was a world war, by 1942, President Roosevelt tried to find an alternative appellation. After rejecting 'the Teutonic Plague' and 'the Tyrants' War', he settled for 'the War of Survival'. But that did not catch on. Finally, in 1945, the US Federal Register announced that, with the approval of President Truman, the late unpleasantness was to be known as **World War II**. In the Soviet Union, the Second World War was known as *Velikaya Otechestvennaya Voyna*, **the Great Fatherland War**. Another name for it there: **the Great Patriotic War**.

One name has not, however, endured – **the Unnecessary War**. In Winston Churchill's preface to *The Gathering Storm*, the first volume of his history of *The Second World War* (1948), he wrote: 'One day President Roosevelt told me that he was asking publicly for suggestions about what the war should be called. I said at once "The Unnecessary War". There never was a war more easy to stop than that which has just wrecked what was left of the world from the previous struggle.'

I think it would be true to say that 'World War I' and 'World War II' are probably the preferred way in the US to refer to what we in the UK still tend to call 'the First World War' and 'the Second World War'. But I may be wrong about this. As for WORLD WAR III, that seems to be an American concept anyway.

On the other hand, some hold that there has only ever been *one* world war to date. A view attributed to Lieut. Col. A.D. Wintle MC (1897–1966) – a brave and gloriously eccentric soldier who fought in both of them – was: 'There's only one war with the Germans. It's lasted thirty years with a lull in the middle while they regrouped.'

In fact, that is a line from a TV film in which he was portrayed by Jim Broadbent. To see if Wintle had actually said any such thing I managed to track down a rare copy of his posthumously published memoir, *The Last Englishman* (1968). All he writes on the matter, when referring to what he usually calls 'the Kaiser's War' and 'Hitler's War', is that they were 'Parts One and Two of the World War'. He then adds: 'Whatever the rest of the world thought, I *knew* that the war with Germany was not over. They were merely lying low … with hindsight I still regard the two world wars as one.' Similarly, in 1941, the cartoonist David Low stated in his foreword to *Europe at War: A History in Sixty Cartoons with a Narrative Text*: 'The war, after an interval of twenty years for a change of moustache, is now resumed.'

*

In the course of writing this book, there are several sources I have made use of and/or to which I refer quite frequently. Sometimes I use these abbreviations:

IHAT	Stuart Berg Flexner, *I Hear America Talking* (1976)
McLaine	Ian McLaine, *Ministry of Morale* (1979)
OED	*The Oxford English Dictionary* (online edn)
Partridge/*Catch Phrases*	Eric Partridge, *A Dictionary of Catch Phrases* (2nd edn, ed. Paul Beale, 1985)
Partridge/*Long Trail*	John Brophy and Eric Partridge, *The Long Trail* (1965 edn) – based on their *Songs and Slang of the British Soldier 1914–18* (1930)
Partridge/*Slang*	Eric Partridge, *A Dictionary of Slang and Unconventional English* (8th edn, ed. Paul Beale, 1984)
Safire	William Safire, *Safire's Political Dictionary* (1978)

Note that the entries are listed in 'letter by letter' order rather than 'word by word' order – that is to say, in alphabetical order of the letters as they appear within the whole phrase exactly as it is written.

Cross-references to other entries are made in SMALL CAPITALS.

There is a keyword index beginning on page 223.

I should like to record my appreciation of the contribution made to this book by several correspondents and contributors to *The Quote ... Unquote Newsletter*, a quarterly electronic publication available from the *Quote ... Unquote* website (www.btwebworld.com/quote-unquote): Marian Bock, Dr John Campbell, Mark English, Howard M. Jones, Joe Kralich, Tony Percy, the late Vernon Noble, and many others. My thanks to them all.

Nigel Rees

(air) ace

'*The air war* and many other of our air warfare terms were coined or popularized by the British in 1915, including: *war ace* or *ace*, a pilot who had shot down at least five enemy planes' – according to *IHAT*. The *OED*, however, defining an 'ace' as 'a crack airman' and providing a citation from *The Times* of 14 September 1917, puts the qualifying tally higher – at 'ten enemy machines'. The origin of the term may lie in its use to describe an 'expert' in late 19th-century America and/or it could reference the ace in a pack of cards.

ack-ack

In telephone communications, a system of pronunciation guides had been established by 1898. The idea was to make clear whichever letter was being spoken and thus to prevent any misunderstanding. Thus, in the First World War, telephone code for the letter 'a' was 'ack', so 'A.A.' – the abbreviation for 'anti-aircraft (gun)' was 'ack-ack' (by 1917). 'Ack' was replaced by 'able' in December 1942, but such a gun was not renamed an 'able-able' ...

action this day

Instruction phrase, for office use, by the time of the Second World War. 'ACTION THIS DAY', 'REPORT IN THREE DAYS' and 'REPORT PROGRESS IN ONE WEEK' were printed tags that Winston Churchill started using in February 1940 to glue on to memos at the Admiralty (where at that time he was First Sea Lord). Subtitled 'Working with

A

Churchill', the book *Action This Day* (1968) is a collection of the reminiscences of those who had been closely associated with Churchill during the Second World War. 'She [Margaret Thatcher] had the draft of that circular on her desk that night. She said "Action this day" and she got it. We didn't stop to argue' – Hugo Young, *One of Us*, Chap. 6 (1989).

Adler Tag [Eagle Day]
This was the German code phrase that would have signalled the invasion of Britain, mooted in 1940 but never launched. The main attack plan was known as *Adlerangriff* [attack of the eagle]. The overall operation was code-named *Seelöwe* [sea lion].

all over by Christmas
At first, it was thought that the European War would not last very long. Having started in August 1914, it would be 'over by Christmas', hence the unofficial, anti-German slogan '**Berlin by Christmas**'. The phrase 'all over by Christmas' was used by some optimists as it had been in several previous wars – none of which was over by the Christmas in question. The fact that this promise was not fulfilled did not prevent Henry Ford from saying, as he tried to stop the war a year later: 'We're going to try to get the boys out of the trenches before Christmas. I've chartered a ship, and some of us are going to Europe.' He was not referring to American boys because the United States had not joined the war at this stage. An alternative version of his statement is: '[The purpose is] to get the boys out of the trenches and **back home by Christmas**.' The *New York*

Tribune announced: 'GREAT WAR ENDS CHRISTMAS DAY. FORD TO STOP IT.'

In her *Autobiography* (1977), Agatha Christie remembered that the South African War would 'all be over in a few weeks'. She went on: 'In 1914 we heard the same phrase, "All over by Christmas". In 1940, "Not much point in storing the carpets with mothballs" – this when the Admiralty took over my house – "It won't last over the winter".' In *Tribune* (28 April 1944), George Orwell recalled a young man 'on the night in 1940 when the big ack-ack barrage was fired over London for the first time', insisting, 'I tell you, it'll all be over by Christmas.' In his diary for 28 November 1950, Harold Nicolson wrote, 'Only a few days ago [General] MacArthur was saying, "Home by Christmas," and now he is saying, "This is a new war [Korea]".' *IHAT* has the comment: '*The war will be over by Christmas* was a popular 1861 expression [in the American Civil War]. Since then several generals and politicians have used the phrase or variations of it, in World War I, World War II, and the Korean war – and none of the wars was over by Christmas.' (Clever-clogs are apt to point out, however, that all wars are eventually over by *a* Christmas ...)

all quiet on the Western Front
A familiar phrase from military communiqués and newspaper reports on the Allied side in the First World War – also taken up jocularly by men in the trenches to describe peaceful inactivity. It was used as the title of the English translation of the novel *Im Westen nichts Neues* [From the Western Front – Nothing to Report] (1929; film US 1930)

A

by the German writer Erich Maria Remarque. The title is ironic – a whole generation was being destroyed while newspapers reported that there was 'no news in the west'. *Partridge/Catch Phrases* hears in it echoes of 'All quiet on the Shipka Pass' – cartoons of the 1877–8 Russo-Turkish War that Partridge says had a vogue in 1915–16, though he never heard the allusion made himself. For no very good reason, Partridge rules out any connection with the American song 'All Quiet Along the Potomac'. This, in turn, came from a poem called 'The Picket Guard' (1861) by Ethel Lynn Beers, a sarcastic commentary on General Brinton McClellan's policy of delay at the start of the Civil War. The phrase (alluding to the Potomac River, which runs through Washington DC) had been used in reports from McLellan's Union headquarters and put in Northern newspaper headlines. 'All quiet along the Potomac' continues to have some use as a portentous way of saying that nothing is happening yet.

(the) Allies

Featuring in both the world wars, these were the forces or states that banded together to fight against the CENTRAL POWERS in the war of 1914–18, or against the AXIS (POWERS) in that of 1939–45. In the First World War, the term was being used in *The Times* by 2 November 1914. The Allies included, at one time or another, Russia (until the Revolution of March 1917), France, the British Commonwealth, Italy, the United States, Japan, Romania, Serbia (defeated in 1915), Belgium, Greece (from July 1917), Portugal and Montenegro (defeated by the end of 1915).

Anderson (shelter)

A British prefabricated air-raid shelter in the Second
World War, named after Sir John Anderson, Home
Secretary and Minister of Home Security (1939–40).
Compare MORRISON SHELTER. It was created by (later Sir)
William Paterson, a Scottish engineer. From the *New
Statesman* 3 June 1939: 'Goats sheltered from high
explosive in Anderson shelters were claimed to be quite
unhurt.' From *War Illustrated* (29 December 1939): 'An
Anderson shelter [is] erected in a kitchen because there is
no garden space available.'

Angel of Death

A nickname bestowed in the Second World War upon
Dr Joseph Mengele, a notorious German concentration-
camp doctor who experimented on inmates – 'for his
power to pick who would live and die in Auschwitz by the
wave of his hand' (*Time* Magazine, 17 June 1985). It is not
clear at what point or by whom this nickname was applied.
'Angel of death' as an expression to describe a bringer of
ills is not a biblical phrase and does not appear to have
arisen until the 18th century. Samuel Johnson used it in
The Rambler in 1752. From Byron's *The Destruction of
Sennacherib* (1815): 'For the Angel of Death spread his
wings on the blast.'

angels one-five

In Royal Air Force jargon, 'angels' means height measured
in units of a thousand feet; 'one-five' stands for fifteen, so
'20 MEs at angels one-five' means 'twenty Messerschmitts

A

at 15,000 feet'. *Angels One Five* was the title of a film (UK 1952) about RAF fighter pilots during the Second World War.

Any gum, chum?
Remark addressed to American GIs based in Britain during the Second World War. 'Crowds of small boys gathered outside American clubs to pester them for gifts, or called out as American lorries passed: "Any gum, chum?" which rapidly became a national catchphrase' – Norman Longmate, *How We Lived Then* (1971).

Anzac
An acronym. 'Anzacs' were members of the Australian and New Zealand Army Corps who fought in the First World War, initially (and especially) at Gallipoli. Anzac Day in both countries is 25 April, commemorating the landing on the beaches there, exposed to Turkish fire, in 1915. The term was first used in military communiqués in that year. Up to that point British troops had tended to use the words 'Aussie' or 'digger', but American forces picked up the new coinage after 1917. Hence, 'Anzac Day' is still used to describe the anniversary of the Gallipoli landings of the Corps on 25 April 1915.

appeasement
A name given to the policy of conciliation and concession towards Nazi Germany, around 1938. The word had, however, been used in this context since the end of the First World War. On 14 February 1920, Winston

Churchill said in a speech: 'I am, and have always been since the firing stopped on November 11, 1918, for a policy of peace, real peace and appeasement.' The word may have become fixed following a letter to *The Times* (4 May 1934) from the 11th Marquess of Lothian: 'The only lasting solution is that Europe should gradually find its way to an internal equilibrium and a limitation of armaments by political appeasement.' Often used disparagingly with reference to the attempts made by Neville Chamberlain, the British Prime Minister, to make a peaceful accommodation with Nazi Germany before the outbreak of war in 1939.

Après la guerre [After the war]

Title phrase from an anonymous song of the First World War sung to the tune of '*Sous les ponts de Paris*'. The first line of each verse is actually '*Après la guerre finie*' [After the war is over] and the song suggests to a Frenchwoman that, as she is in the family way – presumably by a British soldier – they will get married ... after the war is over, i.e., given how long it was lasting, never.

Arbeit macht frei [work makes you free/liberates]

Motto/slogan over the entrance to the Nazi concentration camp at Dachau, Bavaria, by 1933. Also later at Auschwitz, Poland, and other concentration camps.

Are we downhearted? – No!

A morale-boosting phrase connected with the early stages of the First World War but having political origins before that.

A

The politician Joseph Chamberlain said in a 1906 speech: 'We are not downhearted. The only trouble is, we cannot understand what is happening to our neighbours.' The day after he was defeated as candidate in the Stepney Borough Council election of 1909, Clement Attlee, the future Prime Minister, was greeted by a colleague with the cry, 'Are we downhearted?' (He replied, 'Of course we are.') On 18 August 1914, the *Daily Mail* reported: 'For two days the finest troops England has ever sent across the sea have been marching through the narrow streets of old Boulogne in solid columns of khaki ... waving as they say that new slogan of Englishmen: "Are we downhearted? ... Nooooo!" "Shall we win? ... Yessss!"' Florrie Forde sang a song with the phrase as title (written by W. David and Lawrence Wright) in 1914; 'Are We Downhearted?' by Ernest Lees and 'Here We Are, Here We Are, Here We Are Again (The British Army's Battle Cry)' by Charles Wright and Kenneth Lyle were also songs that included the phrase (both also in 1914).

'Arf a mo', Kaiser! [Half a moment/wait a moment, Kaiser!]

The drawing or cartoon by Bert Thomas which had this as caption first appeared in the London *Evening News*, in about 1914. It showed a British 'Tommy' pausing to light his pipe prior to going into action or during a break in it. Subsequently, the drawing may have been used as a 1915–16 recruiting poster. Partridge/*The Long Trail* suggests that a 'half a mo' subsequently became the slang term for a cigarette. A photograph of a handwritten sign from the start of the Second World War shows it declaring, ''Arf a mo, 'itler!' In 1939, there was also a short documentary produced by British Paramount News with the title *'Arf a Mo' Hitler.*

armed neutrality
Though the phrase had existed before – in the 18th century in a Russian context – it was resurrected in the US towards the beginning of the First World War. President Woodrow Wilson proclaimed US neutrality on 19 August 1914. However, both sides in the European War violated American neutrality; the US became pro-Allies and anti-German, and eventually joined the war.

Armistice Day
This designation of the day on which the armistice was concluded and the First World War came to an end – 11 November 1918 – may first have come about in the US on the first anniversary in 1919. Not until 1938, however, did the day become a federal holiday by law. In 1954, the name was changed to 'Veteran's Day' to honour all US veterans including those of the Second World War and the Korean War.

In Britain, perhaps the more frequently used term has been **Armistice Sunday** – for the Sunday closest to 11 November – when commemorations are held at the Cenotaph in London and at war memorials throughout the nation. Since the Second World War, it has been subsumed into **Remembrance Day**. See also TWO MINUTES' SILENCE.

ARP [air-raid precautions]

Though perhaps more closely associated with the Second
World War, this official term for measures to limit the risk
of air raids, or the damage they might cause, was in use
early in the First World War. A heading in *The Times* on
24 June 1915 was: 'Air-raid Precautions. Use And Abuse Of
The Fire Alarm'. By 1924, a department of the Home Office
with this name (though usually referred to by its initials)
had been created to organize the protection of civilians from
air raids. By 1937, *The Lancet* was commenting: 'A.R.P. These
sinister initials are being made more and more familiar by a
spate of books on air-raid precautions.' By 1939, the term
had been officially superseded by 'Civil Defence', though as
The Times Weekly observed on 6 September (note the date,
just five days after the war officially began): 'It is impossible
now to say where air-raid precautions end and where civil
defence begins.' 'ARP' lived on in popular parlance but after
1945 gave way completely to 'Civil Defence'.

arsenal of democracy

Phrase used by President Franklin D. Roosevelt in a radio
'fireside chat' on 29 December 1940, one year before the US
entered the Second World War: 'We must be the great
arsenal of democracy.'

Asdic

Acronym for 'Anti-Submarine Detection and Investigation
Committee' – an early British sonar/echo-sounding device
for locating enemy submarines, introduced in the First
World War. In December 1939, *War Illustrated* was reporting:

'Asdic … mentioned by Mr. Churchill in one of his speeches … [is] a type of secret apparatus now used by the Navy.'

Auf nach Berlin [On to Berlin]
A German nationalist cry current from 1919–24.

AWOL [absent without leave]
Unwarranted absence from the military for a short period, but falling short of actual desertion. The acronym dates from the American Civil War, when offenders had to wear a placard with these initials printed on it. During the First World War, the initials were still being pronounced individually. Not until just before the Second World War was it pronounced as the acronym 'AWOL'. The term does not mean 'absent without *official* leave', indeed sometimes it was just put as 'A.W.L.' This form of the abbreviation may have been more popular with the British and Australian armies; 'AWOL' with the Americans.

Axis (Powers)
Originally there were only two in the Second World War – Germany and Italy. 'The name was coined and made common by Mussolini who, after signing an agreement with Hitler in 1936, called Berlin and Rome "an axis around which all European states … can assemble"' – *IHAT*. Finally, the 'enemy' powers included Germany, Italy, Japan, Bulgaria, Hungary, Romania and Finland (though the latter never declared war on the US). 'The "Rome-Berlin axis" is a conceit which has its momentary attractions' – *The Times* (3 November 1936).

Axis Sally

Nickname of Mildred Gillars (1900–88), an American citizen who went to Germany to study in the 1930s and took a job as an announcer with Radio Berlin in 1940. She broadcast propaganda to the Allies and was given her nickname by American troops – though the name was also applied to Rita Zucca, who broadcast from Italy. After the war was over, Gillars was repatriated to the US and given a long prison term for treason.

back home
How American forces in the First World War referred to the US. The British more usually referred to their home country as BLIGHTY.

back home by Christmas
See ALL OVER BY CHRISTMAS.

backroom boys
Nickname given to scientists and boffins who did secret research – and specifically to those who were relied on to produce inventions and new gadgets for weaponry and navigation in the Second World War. Compare *The Small Back Room*, title of a novel (1943) by Nigel Balchin that dealt with such people. The phrase was originated, in this sense, by Lord Beaverbrook as Minister of Aircraft Production when he paid tribute to his research department in a broadcast on 19 March 1941: 'Let me say that the credit belongs to the boys in the backrooms [*sic*]. It isn't the man who sits in the limelight who should have the praise. It is not the men who sit in prominent places. It is the men in the backrooms.' In the US, the phrase 'backroom boys' can be traced to the 1870s at least, but Beaverbrook can be credited with the modern application to scientists and boffins. The inspiration quite obviously was Beaverbrook's favourite film *Destry Rides Again* (1939) in which Marlene Dietrich jumped on the bar of the Last Chance Saloon and sang the Frank Loesser song 'See What

the Boys in the Back Room Will Have'. According to A.J.P. Taylor, Beaverbrook believed that 'Dietrich singing the Boys in the Backroom is a greater work of art than the Mona Lisa'. Also in 1941, Edmund Wilson entitled a book (otherwise unconnected), *The Boys in the Back Room: Notes on California Novelists*. A British film with Arthur Askey was entitled *Back Room Boy* in 1942.

An even earlier appearance of the bar phrase occurs in the Marx Brothers film *Animal Crackers* (1930): 'Let's go and see what the boys in the backroom will have.' In 1924, Dorothy Parker is said to have cabled to her friends at the Round Table concerning the flop of a show she had written with Elmer Rice: 'Close Harmony did a cool ninety dollars at the matinee. Ask the boys in the backroom what they will have.' So obviously it was already a well-established phrase in the old sense.

backs to the land

'Back to the land' was a political slogan of the 1890s when it was realized that the Industrial Revolution and the transfer of the population towards non-agricultural labour had starved farming of workers. In the 1970s, a TV comedy series was called *Backs to the Land*, playing on the phrase to provide an innuendo about its heroines, 'Land Girls' – members of the Women's Land Army conscripted to work on the land during the Second World War (though the W.L.A. was first established in the First World War). Norman Longmate noted in *How We Lived Then* (1971): 'The rumour that their motto was "Backs to the land" was an early wartime witticism'.

backs to the wall

The expression 'backs to the wall', meaning 'up against it', dates back to 1535, at least, but it was memorably used when the Germans launched their last great offensive of the First World War. On 12 April 1918, Sir Douglas Haig, as British Commander-in-Chief on the Western Front, issued an order for his troops to stand firm: 'There is no other course open to us but to fight it out. Every position must be held to the last man: there must be no retirement. With our backs to the wall and believing in the justice of our cause each one of us must fight on to the end. The safety of our homes and the Freedom of mankind alike depend upon the conduct of each one of us at this critical moment.' A.J.P. Taylor in his *English History 1914–1945* (1966) comments: 'In England this sentence was ranked with Nelson's last message. At the front, the prospect of staff officers fighting with their backs to the walls of their luxurious châteaux had less effect.'

(to) bail out

To escape from a damaged aircraft by jumping out and using a parachute. The verb seems to have been an American coinage and first recorded in about 1930.

(the) balloon's gone up

Current by 1924 and meaning 'action has commenced', particularly in a military sense. The expression may derive from the letting go of balloons to mark the start of festivities generally or perhaps from the sending up of barrage balloons (introduced during the First World War)

B

to protect targets from air raids. The fact that these balloons – or manned observation balloons – had 'gone up' would signal that some form of action was imminent. C.H. Rolph, in *London Particulars* (1980), suggests that the expression was in use earlier than this, by 1903–4.

Banzai! [(May you live) ten thousand years!]

From a hundred war films and cheap comics we are familiar with the cry used by Japanese forces in the Second World War. Addressed to the Emperor, wishing him long life, the cry was recorded by the 1890s. M.R. Lewis observed (1986): 'The root of the problem is that a language written in the Chinese ideographic characters is often difficult to translate sensibly into a West European language, because it is often not apparent when the literal meaning is intended and when the figurative. "*Banzai*" literally means no more than "ten thousand years", but what it more usually means is "for a long time". So, a pen in Japanese is, when literally translated, a "ten thousand year writing brush", which is gibberish in any language! What it actually means is "a long-lasting writing instrument" … For the suicide pilots, the ritual shout of "*Banzai!*" swept up many layers of meaning, of which the most immediate was undoubtedly "*Tenno heika banzai*" – "Long live the Emperor", a phrase which goes back into the mists of Japanese history, despite its appropriation by the nationalist movements of the 1930s. The phrase is still in use on such occasions as the Emperor's birthday, as I can testify from recent experience. When he stepped out on to the balcony and the shouts rose around me, I began to feel that I was in the wrong movie! As for the

oddity of the phrase – if literally translated, is it really so different from: "Zadok the priest, and Nathan the prophet, anointed Solomon king. And all the people rejoiced and said, God save the king. Long live the king, *may the king live for ever*. Amen. Alleluia" – which has been sung at the coronation of almost every English sovereign since William of Normandy was crowned in Westminster Abbey on Christmas Day 1066.'

Jonathan Swift includes 'May you live a thousand years' among the conversational chestnuts in *Polite Conversation* (1738). The Sergeant in Charles Dickens's *Great Expectations*, Chap. 5 (1860–1) incorporates it in a toast.

basket case

This phrase now has two applications – firstly, to describe a mental or physical cripple and, secondly, a totally ruined enterprise. Either way, it seems to be an American term and the *OED*'s earliest citation is from the *U.S. Official Bulletin* (28 March 1919) in the aftermath of the First World War: 'The Surgeon General of the Army ... denies ... that there is any foundation for the stories that have been circulated ... of the existence of "basket cases" in our hospitals.' Indeed, another definition of the term is 'a soldier who has lost all four limbs' – thus, presumably, requiring transportation in something like a basket. To complicate matters, Stuart Berg Flexner, the American word expert, describes this as being originally *British* Army slang. It has been suggested, probably misguidedly, that the association with mental disability comes from the fact that basket-weaving is an activity sometimes carried out in mental hospitals.

The second meaning was established by about 1973 and is still frequently used in business journalism describing doomed ventures: 'On a continent that is full of economic basket cases, the small, landlocked nation is virtually debt free' (*Newsweek*, 11 January 1982).

Here, one might guess that the original phrase has been hijacked and the implication changed. What the writer is now referring to is something that is so useless that it is fit only to be thrown into a waste-paper basket.

Battle of Britain

The urge to give names to battles – even before they are fought and won – is well exemplified by Winston Churchill's coinage of 18 June 1940: 'What General Weygand called the Battle of France is over. I expect that the Battle of Britain is about to begin.'

It duly became the name by which the decisive overthrowing of German invasion plans by 'the Few' is known. The order of the day, read aloud to every pilot on 10 July, contained the words: 'The Battle of Britain is about to begin. Members of the Royal Air Force, the fate of generations is in your hands.'

In his biography of Churchill (2001), Roy Jenkins credits a 32-page Air Ministry booklet of March 1941 with putting the name 'Battle of Britain' into general circulation, without mentioning that Churchill had used the phrase in his famous 1940 speech.

Another Churchill coinage – 'the Battle of Egypt' (speech, 10 November 1942) – caught on less well.

Battle of the Atlantic

Name given to 'the long battle by US and British cargo ships, convoys, destroyers, and planes against German submarines and bombers to keep the Atlantic open, so that weapons and supplies could reach England from America. The term was coined by the First Lord of the Admiralty, A.V. Alexander, on March 15, 1941. The battle for control of the North Atlantic began in September, 1939, and was all but over by 1943, when Allied detecting devices, destroyers, and planes stopped our heavy losses to the Germans' – *IHAT*.

Battle of the Bulge

'After D-Day the Allied invading forces advanced steadily into Europe. Then on December 16, 1944, the Germans launched their final counterattack of the war. This attack created a "bulge" 60 miles [96km] deep in the Belgium-Luxembourg sector of the Allied lines, trapping US forces in the snow-filled Ardennes forest … The "bulge" was straightened in January, 1945, and the Allied advance continued' – *IHAT*.

(A) bayonet is a weapon with a worker at each end

A British pacifist slogan from 1940, quoted in *The Penguin Dictionary of Modern Quotations* (1971).

Be like Dad – keep Mum

A slogan coined by the Ministry of Information in about 1941. The security theme was paramount in wartime propaganda. Civilians as well as military personnel were urged not to talk about war-related matters lest the enemy somehow got to hear. A similar slogan was **'Keep Mum, she's not so dumb!'**

This appeared on a poster showing an elegant, very un-Mum-like blonde being ogled by representatives of the three Armed Services. Both these derive ultimately from 'mum's the word', a warning or exhortation meaning 'keep silent on this matter'. No mother is being invoked here: 'mum' is just a representation of 'mmmm', the noise made when lips are sealed. The word 'mumble' obviously derives from the same source. Shakespeare has the idea in *Henry VI, Part 2*, I.ii.89 (1590): 'Seal up your lips and give no words but mum'. The phrase had been known since 1540.

beachhead
'The initial amphibious landing site which had to be "secured" from its defenders before additional troops and supplies were landed' – *IHAT*. The *OED* comments that the word (also in the form 'beach-head') is 'illogically formed' in imitation of 'bridge-head' and defines it, rather, as 'a fortified position of troops landed on a beach.' By 1940.

Beast of Belsen
A name given to Josef Kramer, German Commandant of the Belsen concentration camp during the worst period of its history, from December 1944 to the end of the Second World War. He was executed for his crimes in 1945.

BEF [British Expeditionary Force]
The BEF landed in France on 7 August 1914. Why 'expeditionary'? Presumably because the Force set out with a specific purpose – rather the like the 'task force' in the much later Falklands conflict – and because at that stage in

the war, people shrank from any talk of an 'army'. The AEF
(American Expeditionary Force) reached France on 25 June
1917. The term 'BEF' was resurrected at the start of the
Second World War. It was the BEF that had to be rescued
from Dunkirk.

(You will be home) before the leaves have fallen from the trees

Kaiser Wilhelm II said this to German troops leaving for
the Front in August 1914 at the beginning of the First
World War. After that, it was going to be 'ALL OVER BY
CHRISTMAS', but it dragged on for four years. Quoted in
Barbara Tuchman, *The Guns of August*, Chap. 9 (1962).

Belgium put the kibosh on the Kaiser

The expression 'to put the kibosh/kybosh on to something'
means 'to put a stop to, or frustrate, an attempted action'
and has been known since the 19th century. The word
'kibosh' is of uncertain origin but Partridge/*Slang* offers the
suggestion that it may derive from the Yiddish *kabas*,
kabbasten, meaning 'to suppress'. The lyric for the anti-
German First World War song 'Belgium Put the Kibosh on
the Kaiser' was written by Alf Ellerton and published in
1915. The chorus is:

> For Belgium put the kibosh on the Kaiser
> Europe took the stick and made him sore;
> On his throne it hurts to sit,
> And when John Bull starts to hit,
> He will never sit upon it any more.

Berlin by Christmas!

See ALL OVER BY CHRISTMAS.

(And the) best of British luck!

In his autobiography, *On the Way I Lost It* (1976), the comedian Frankie Howerd wrote: 'The phrase is so common now that I frequently surprise people when I tell them it was my catchphrase on *Variety Bandbox* [BBC radio comedy show, late 1940s].' Partridge/*Catch Phrases* suggests, however, that the 'British luck' version had already been a Second World War army phrase meaning the exact opposite of what it appeared to say, and compares it with a line from the First World War song 'MADEMOISELLE FROM ARMENTIÈRES', some versions of which contain the line: 'Over the top with the best of luck / Parlay-voo'.

Bevin boys

Young men in the UK who were directed to work in the coal mines during the Second World War instead of being conscripted into the Services. The measure was introduced in 1942 by Ernest Bevin, Minister of Labour and National Service, hence the name. The 'boys' were selected by ballot.

Big Bertha

Soldiers' nickname for the German long-range gun in the First World War that was used to shell Paris in 1918. However, a mortar of 42cm (16¼in) was being made at the Krupp works by 1914 and was baptized 'Bertha die fleissige' (Bertha, the Zealous). Bertha, the only child of Friedrich

Alfred Krupp (1854–1902), inherited the great engineering and armaments undertaking and owned it from 1903 to 1943. Her husband became head of the firm, which produced much of the weaponry used on the German side in the war. 'Big Bertha spoke for the first time on March 23, and at the sound of her voice Paris was intensely surprised' – *The Sphere* (20 July 1918).

Big Four
Britain, France, Italy and the United States – the four countries that eventually led the ALLIES during the First World War.

big lie [after German *große Lüge*]
In his book *Mein Kampf* (1925), Adolf Hitler wrote: 'The size of a lie is a definite factor in causing it to be believed … The primitive simplicity of [the minds of the great masses of the people means they] … will more easily fall victims to a big lie than to a small one.' Hence, in Nazi propaganda, a lie that was so huge was thought able to take in the public even if it was unsupported factually.

Big Three
Churchill, Roosevelt and Stalin, heads of government of the UK, US and USSR respectively in the Second World War, so dubbed when they met in conference at Yalta in 1945. The term had also been applied to the American, British and French leaders – Woodrow Wilson, David Lloyd George and Georges Clemenceau – at the 1919 Versailles Peace Conference.

Bitch of Buchenwald

Nickname of Ilse Koch (1906–suicide 1967), wife of the
Commandant of Buchenwald, a Nazi concentration camp
during the Second World War. Also known as the Beast
of Buchenwald and perhaps originally as the Witch of
Buchenwald, after the German *die Hexe von Buchenwald.*
Notorious for her sadistic abuse of inmates, she may never,
however, have actually had anyone killed so that their
interesting tattoos could be preserved and the skin turned
into lampshades.

Black Jack

Nickname of US General John Joseph Pershing
(1860–1948), Commander-in-Chief of the American
Expeditionary Force in the First World War.

black market

During the Second World War, this term originally referred
to the illicit trade in stolen military supplies but then was
extended to include all sorts of illegal buying and selling
of 'rationed, scarce and price-controlled items', e.g. clothes,
food, petrol and so on. The term had been used somewhat
in the First World War, derived from the German
Schwarzmarkt.

blackout

The period of darkness when no lights were to be displayed
for fear of attracting enemy bombers. It was particularly
widespread and severe in the Second World War, when
blinds and curtains were drawn over windows, car and

street lamps were masked, and wardens made inspections to ensure that no glimmer of light could be seen from above. The term was established by the time of this report in *The Lancet* (3 August 1935): 'Mr Harcourt Johnstone asked the Prime Minister whether instructions for compulsory "black-outs" in districts where experiments were being carried out against air attacks were issued by authority of any Government department.'

Blighty

British soldiers serving abroad during the First World War referred to England or home as 'Blighty'. Established by 8 October 1915, when *The Times* (weekly edition) had: 'The only thing they looked forward to was getting back to "Blighty" again.' There was a popular song written by A.J. Mills, Fred Godfrey and Bennett Scott (1916) of which the chorus was: 'Take me back to dear old Blighty! / Put me on the train for London town! / Take me anywhere / Drop me ANYWHERE, / Liverpool, Leeds, or Birmingham, well, I don't care.' It ended: 'Tiddley iddley ighty, / Hurry me home to Blighty, / Blighty is the place for me!' The word is said to derive from slightly earlier usage in the Indian army. *Bilāyati* is Hindustani for 'foreign' and had come to mean 'European' or 'English'. A 'blighty wound' was one severe enough to take the soldier back to Britain for treatment and then convalescence.

blimp

When used to describe a type of stupid, reactionary, elderly gentleman, this name derives from the cartoon character

Colonel Blimp, created between the wars by David Low, and
who reached a kind of apotheosis in the film *The Life and
Death of Colonel Blimp* (1943). The character, in turn, took
his name from an experimental airship/balloon developed
during the First World War (by 1916). Without frames and
thus 'non-ridi', these were described as 'limp'. There was an
'A-limp' and a 'B-limp'. The aviator Horace Short may have
been the man who dubbed them 'blimps'.

Another suggestion is that the name is onomatopoeic.
In 1915, a Lt. Cunningham of the Royal Navy Air Service is
said to have flicked his thumb against the surface of one of
the airships and imitated the odd noise thus produced.
Alternatively, J.R.R. Tolkien, writing in 1926, hazarded a
guess that the name derived from a mixture of 'blister' and
'lump', both of which the balloons resembled, adding that
'the vowel *i* not *u* was chosen because of its diminutive
significance typical of war-humour.'

(the) Blitz
A sudden and concentrated attack by ground and/or air
forces as practised by the Germans in the Second World
War, from *Blitzkrieg*, 'lightning war'. The term was most
commonly used for Luftwaffe bombing attacks on London
and other cities in 1940–41. Shortened to *Blitz* by 1940.
From the *Daily Express* (9 September 1940): 'Blitz bombing
of London goes on all night.'

blockbusters
Nickname given by RAF crews in the Second World War to
the heavier bombs that could be carried when Halifax and

Lancaster four-engine bombers came into service, especially the first 4,000-pounders (1814kg); followed by even more devastating 'cookies'. Perhaps derived from their capability of destroying a whole block of buildings. By 1942.

blood, toil, tears and sweat

'I would say to the House, as I said to those who have joined this Government: I have nothing to offer but blood, toil, tears and sweat' – from Winston Churchill's speech to the House of Commons (13 May 1940) upon becoming Prime Minister. Note the order of the last five words. There are echoes in these of earlier speeches and writings. The combination makes an appearance in John Donne's line from *An Anatomy of the World* (1611): ''Tis in vain to do so or mollify it with thy tears or sweat or blood.' Byron follows with 'blood, sweat and tear-wrung millions' in 1823. Theodore Roosevelt spoke in an 1897 speech of 'the blood and sweat and tears, the labour and the anguish, through which, in the days that have gone, our forefathers moved to triumph'. The more usual order of the words was later enshrined in the name of the 1970s American band Blood, Sweat and Tears. Churchill seemed to avoid this configuration, however. In 1931, he had already written of the Tsarist armies: 'Their sweat, their tears, their blood bedewed the endless plain.'

Possibly the closest forerunner of Churchill's 'backs to the wall' exhortation was Giuseppe Garibaldi's impromptu speech to his followers on 2 July 1849, before Rome fell to French troops. The speech was not taken down at the time, so this version is made up of various accounts. Seated upon a horse in the Piazza of St Peter's, he declared: 'Fortune, who betrays us today, will smile on us tomorrow. I am going out from Rome. Let those who wish to continue the war against the stranger, come with me. I offer neither pay, nor quarters, nor provisions; I offer hunger, thirst, forced marches, battles and death [*fame, sete, marcie forzate, battaglie e morte*]. Let him who loves his country with his heart, and not merely his lips, follow me.' As precedents go, this is obviously quite a close one, and it is probable that Churchill had read G.M. Trevelyan's series of books about Garibaldi, published at the turn of the century, in which the lines occur. Having launched such a famous phrase, Churchill referred to it five more times during the course of the war, though he did not always use all four keywords or in the original order.

Indeed, right from the start, people seem to have had difficulty in getting the order of the words right. The natural inclination is to put 'blood', 'sweat' and 'tears' together. Joan Wyndham in *Love Lessons – A Wartime Diary* (1985) concludes her entry for 13 May 1940 with: 'Later we listened to a very stirring speech by Churchill about "blood, toil, sweat and tears".' There is a slight suspicion that this diary may have been 'improved' somewhat in the editing, but not, obviously, to the point of imposing accuracy. Boller and George's *They Never Said It* (1989), dedicated to exposing quotation errors, has Churchill saying 'blood *and* toil, tears and sweat'.

Boche/Fritz/Hun/Jerry/Kraut

Abusive names for the Germans and specifically German soldiers during the First World War, though they were all already well-established usages by 1914. Only 'Jerry' really survived into the Second World War. According to Richard Hillary, *The Last Enemy* (1942), a London taxi driver used the term typically to him during the Blitz: 'Jerry's wasting 'is time trying to break our morale, when 'e might be doing some real damage on some small town.'

'Boche' comes via French, where it is short for *allboche* (a combination of *allemand* + *caboche* = German blockhead) by 1887. From the *Daily Express* (30 September 1914): 'Monsieur had better come under cover. The "Bosches" are still firing this way.' Partridge/*Long Trail* suggests this word was never used by the 'other ranks', who preferred the following:

- 'Fritz', the German nickname for *Friedrich* (Frederick).
- 'Jerry', which derives from the British slang for chamber pot. German helmets were thought to resemble them. But if spelt 'Gerry', might relate to '*Ger*man'.
- 'Hun', which derives from the name of 4th- and 5th-century invaders, led by Attila the Hun (in use by 1908). The immediate source of the application of 'Hun' to the Germans was the speech delivered by Wilhelm II to the German troops about to sail for China on 27 July 1900.
- 'Kraut', which comes from the German word *Kraut*, meaning 'herb, vegetable, cabbage'. By 1918.

boffin

A scientist or inventor, probably of RAF origin in the Second World War but adopted in other Services. Such men produced navigational aids and bomb-aiming and gunnery gadgetry. Of unclear origin, but there was an eccentric gentleman called 'Mr Boffin' in Dickens's *Our Mutual Friend*.

bogeys

The 'blips' on a radar screen that denoted enemy aircraft (from 1939), marking them off from 'our own' bombers and fighters by 'iff' (identification, friend or foe).

bomber

This word for a plane that dropped bombs came into use back in 1915.

Bomber Harris

Nickname of Marshal of the Royal Air Force, Sir Arthur Harris Bt. (1882–1984), aggressive Commander-in-Chief of Bomber Command in the Second World War. An advocate of STRATEGIC BOMBING, he directed the great bombing offensive from Britain, a relentless night-by-night attack on German cities and manufacturing centres, ports and railways, and on other enemy territory. His policy has since been criticized and its effects questioned. Known as 'Butch' or 'Bert' to his colleagues, the 'Bomber' bit came from a more public perception.

(The) bomber will always get through

Phrase from a speech made to the House of Commons (10 November 1932) by Stanley Baldwin (1867–1947), the de facto Prime Minister. This remark has to be seen in the context of the times – the First World War had introduced the completely new concept of airborne bombardment. Said Baldwin in full: 'I think it is well for the man in the street to realize that there is no power on earth that can protect him from being bombed. Whatever people may tell him, the bomber will always get through. The only defence is in offence, which means that you have to kill more women and children more quickly than the enemy if you want to save yourselves.' In a later speech to the House of Commons (30 July 1934) Baldwin provided a corollary: 'Since the day of the air, the old frontiers are gone. When you think of the chalk cliffs of Dover, you think of the Rhine. That is where our frontier lies.'

boondocks/boonies
Somewhere obscure, out of the way and 'in the sticks'. During the Second World War, American GIs stationed in the Philippines were sometimes sent to the mountain regions. *Bundok* means 'mountain' in Tagalog, the official language of the Philippines. By 1944.

brass hat
A high-ranking officer in the British Army (or other Service), so called after the gilt insignia on his cap. In common use by the time of the First World War but had been known since at least 1893 (Kipling). A coinage possibly influenced by the American term 'brass button brigade', referring to top Army and Navy officials in Washington, who in turn became 'the brass' or 'the war brass' during the Spanish-American War (1898).

Britain can take it
A morale-boosting slogan from the Ministry of Information in 1940. It was used (with an exclamation mark) as the title of one of the Ministry's propaganda films, released in that

year and showing the courage with which the population of London was facing the Blitz. In fact, it was a shorter version of *London Can Take It*, in which the American journalist Quentin Reynolds gave President Roosevelt the kind of material he needed to swing American popular opinion behind Britain's war effort.

Slogans rained down upon the hapless British as profusely as German bombs during the Second World War. The Ministry of Information, in blunderbuss fashion, fired away with as much material as possible in the hope of hitting something at some point. Some of the slogans were brilliant; others were quite the reverse – like this one. 'While the public appreciated due recognition of their resolute qualities, they resented too great an emphasis on the stereotyped image of the Britisher in adversity as a wise-cracking Cockney. They were irritated by propaganda which represented their grim experience as a sort of particularly torrid Rugby match' (*McLaine*). Hence, the Ministry's abandonment of this slogan in December 1940.

Winston Churchill seems, wisely, not to have used the 'Britain can take it' approach, though in one of his victory speeches in May 1945 he did quote '**London can take it**'. According to Richard Hillary, *The Last Enemy* (1942), that version 'was already becoming a truism' by the end of 1940.

Bullfrog of the Pontine Marshes
Benito Mussolini (1883–1945), the Italian dictator, so named derisively by Winston Churchill in the Second World War.

Bundles for Britain
Name of an American organization founded by Mrs Wales
Latham (and sponsored by Mrs Winston Churchill) in
January 1940, to send bundles of food and clothing to
English civilians.

B.U.R.M.A. [Be upstairs/undressed ready my angel]
Lovers' acronym in correspondence, used to avoid military
censorship. Partridge/*Slang* dates this from the time of the
Second World War.

Business as usual
This now standard declaration posted when a shop or office
has suffered some misfortune like a fire or is undergoing
alterations was known by 1884. In the First World War,
H.E. Morgan (later Sir Herbert Morgan) was an advertising
consultant to H. Gordon Selfridge, the London store owner.
On 26 August 1914, Selfridge said: ' "Business As Usual"
must be the order of the day.' In a Guildhall speech on 9
November, Winston Churchill said: 'The maxim of the
British people is "Business as usual".' Morgan worked for
W.H. Smith & Sons as well, which also promoted the slogan.
It had quite a vogue until it was proved manifestly untrue
and hopelessly inappropriate.

Butcher of Lyons
This nickname was given to Klaus Barbie (1913–91), head of
the German Gestapo in Lyons from 1942 to 1944, who was
so called because of his alleged cruelty, torture, and murder
of French Resistance fighters and others. Twice tried *in*

absentia, Barbie was brought back to Lyons from exile in Bolivia in 1983 and tried again in 1987. Patrick Marnham, in the *Independent* (18 March 1987), protested that Barbie had never been known thus in Lyons and that his nickname there was 'Le Bourreau' [the executioner].

buzz bomb

Another name for the 'flying bombs' that were launched by the Germans against London and other cities from September 1944 (i.e. after D-DAY). There were two types – the V-1 and the V-2, following their German name *Vergektungswaffe* [retaliation weapon]. The V-1 was in essence a small, pilotless plane whose engine made a buzzing noise. The V-2 was more of a rocket.

Careless talk costs lives

Security slogan, during the Second World War in the UK,
from mid-1940. Devised by Harold Grigsby (1903–95),
according to his *Daily Telegraph* obituary, it became the
most enduring of security slogans on posters.

This was especially so when it was accompanied by
Fougasse cartoons – showing two men in a club, for
example, one saying to the other ' … strictly between
four walls' (behind them is a painting through which
Hitler's head is peeping), or two women gossiping in
front of Hitler wallpaper (with the additional slogan,
'Don't forget that WALLS HAVE EARS!') Another Fougasse
cartoon (dating from 1940) had two foreign military
types (possibly Hitler and Mussolini) sitting behind
gossiping women on a bus or train. Here the slogan
'You never know <u>who's</u> listening!' is coupled with
'Careless talk costs lives'.

A poster showing simply a woman's hat was coupled
with the slogan 'KEEP IT UNDER YOUR HAT!'

carpet bombing

The dropping of a large concentration of bombs to cause
extensive and widespread damage to an area. On 26 January
1944, *The New York Times* was reporting that: 'Marshal
Coningham evolved a system of "carpet bombing" in which
bomb bursts covered the German positions in advance of
attacks by tanks and infantry.'

Carrots keep you healthy and help you to see in the blackout

According to a carrot website: 'Carrots were one vegetable which was in plentiful supply and as a result were widely utilized as a substitute for scarce foodstuffs and used in several "mock" recipes. It was also a major ingredient of the campaign called Dig for Victory, which was extensively publicized with songs and posters featuring Dr Carrot and Potato Pete. It was run for most of the war by Professor John Raeburn, a respected agricultural economist, who joined the Ministry of Food in 1939 as a statistician and two years later was appointed to lead the Agricultural Plans Branch. While much of the credit for the campaign went to Lord Woolton, the Minister of Food from 1940 to 1943, Mr Raeburn ran it until the end of the war and was responsible for its continuing success. At one point there was a glut of carrots, and the Government let it be known that carotene, which is believed to help night vision, was largely responsible for the RAF's increasing success in shooting down enemy bombers.' This was parodied in 'The Aftermyth of War', a sketch in the revue *Beyond the Fringe* (1961): 'Mr Charles Spedding of Hoxton remembers … "I was always out in the garden round about nineish planting out some carrots for the night fighters … "'

Cat's Eyes

Nickname of Group Captain John Cunningham (1917–2002), distinguished RAF night fighter pilot in the Second World War. Even when navigational aids were not available, he managed to shoot down some twelve German aircraft.

'Cat's eyes', the light-reflecting studs used to demarcate traffic lanes on roads at night, had been introduced in the early 1930s, as an improvement on simply following the white line painted down the middle of the road.

C'est la guerre! [That's war!]
An exclamation from the First World War, used to cover disappointment at the machinations of fate or at the failure of anything. Compare the much later 'That's show business!'

Central Powers
Germany, Austro-Hungary, Turkey and Bulgaria – in the First World War. These countries opposed the ALLIES and were so called because of their geographical location in Central Europe.

Chamberlain's umbrella
Of Prime Ministerial props in the twentieth century, one thinks of Churchill's cigars, Baldwin's and Wilson's pipes, and Chamberlain's umbrella. At the time of the Munich Agreement, Chips Channon noted in his diary (28 September 1938): 'The Saviour of Peace got quietly into his car, umbrella and all', and later referred to Chamberlain as 'Old Brolly'.

Chindits
A Long-Range Penetration Force, commanded by Major-General Orde Wingate, operating behind the Japanese lines in Burma during the Second World War, making long marches or landing in gliders. These Allied

C

troops, carrying out daring raids, adopted a Burmese dragon-like device – the *chinthé* – as their emblem.

When Churchill reported their exploits to the American President, Roosevelt described them as 'an epic of achievement for the airborne troops, not forgetting the mules'. By 1943.

civvies
Civilian clothes as opposed to military uniform. From about 1889, but popular in the First and Second World Wars.

Cliveden Set
In so far as it existed, the set was in favour of APPEASEMENT and took its name from the Buckinghamshire seat of Lord and Lady Astor, who were at the centre of it, in the 1930s. The name first appeared in Claud Cockburn's news sheet *The Week* (17 June 1936). Chips Channon wrote in his diary on 4 April 1938 (of a reception given by Lady Astor): 'The function will be criticised, since there is already talk of a so-called "Cliveden" set which is alleged to be pro-Hitler, but which, in reality, is only pro-Chamberlain and pro-sense.' On 8 May 1940, Channon added: 'I think [Lady Astor] is seriously rattled by the "Cliveden Set" allegations which were made against her before the war, and now wants to live them down.'

CO
Abbreviation in both world wars for either 'Commanding Officer' or 'conscientious objector' – in the first sense since 1889 and in the second by 1916.

collaborators

Second World War term for those – especially in occupied
France – who cooperated and worked with the Germans.
From the *New Statesman* (25 September 1943): 'Infiltration
would be easy with the help of such well-placed collaborators.'

Come on you sons of bitches, do you want to live forever?

According to *IHAT*, US Marine Sergeant Daniel Daly
(1874–1937) is remembered for having shouted this during
Allied resistance at the Battle of Belleau Wood in June 1918
(during the First World War). H.L. Mencken, in his
dictionary of quotations (1942), has it from 'an American
sergeant ... addressing soldiers reluctant to make a charge',
in the form: 'What's the matter with you guys? Do you want
to live forever?' Otherwise the saying remains untraced.

Whatever the case, Daly was not the first military man
to use this form of encouragement. Frederick the Great
(1712–86) demanded of hesitating guards at Kolin (18 June
1757), '*Ihr Racker/Hunde, wollt ihr ewig* [or *immer*] *leben?*
[Rascals/Dogs, would you live forever?]'. Mencken
concludes that the cry is 'probably ancient', anyway.

'Comin' in on a Wing and a Prayer'

A popular US song of the Second World War (published in
1943) supposedly took its title from a remark by an actual
pilot who was coming in to land with a badly damaged
plane. Harold Adamson and Jimmy McHugh's lyrics include
the lines: 'Tho' there's one motor gone, we can still carry on
/ Comin' in on a Wing and a Pray'r.' A film about life on an

American aircraft carrier (US 1944) was called simply *Wing and a Prayer*.

concentration camp
Name given to a type of German prison camp in the Second World War. It also covers the Nazi extermination camps where six million Jews were put to death during what came to be called the HOLOCAUST. The term had been in use, however, since Spain had its 'reconcentration camps' in the 1890s and Lord Kitchener established 'concentration camps' for South Africans in 1899–1902, during the Boer War. These were places where those civilians who might give aid and succour to rebels and guerillas were 'concentrated' under the control of Government troops.

convoy
Since the 15th century, the verb 'to convoy' has meant 'to escort or accompany'. From the end of the First World War, the noun 'convoy' was used to describe a fleet of merchant and/or troop ships protected from submarines by cruisers and destroyers.

Coughs and sneezes spread diseases
A Ministry of Health warning from about 1942, coupled with the line, 'Trap the germs in your handkerchief.' A poster had the words 'Ministry of Health says …' – and the slogan – accompanying a spread handkerchief on which an H.M. Bateman cartoon was clipped. It showed a man sneezing all over another man and his food in a cafeteria queue. Other versions had a similar message.

(A) country fit for heroes
See (A) LAND FIT FOR HEROES.

(the) cruel sea
According to more than one source, Nicholas Monsarrat derived the title of his 1951 novel *The Cruel Sea* from Captain Gilbert Roberts of the Royal Navy, who said: 'It is the war of the little ships and the lonely aircraft, long patient and unpublicized, our two great enemies – the U-Boats and the Cruel Sea.' The novel (filmed in 1951) is a bleak look at life and death on board ships during the BATTLE OF THE ATLANTIC. However, Winston Churchill had already used the phrase in *The World Crisis*, Pt 3, Chap. 9 (1923–9): 'And indeed the spectacle of helpless merchant seamen, their barque shattered and foundering, left with hard intention by fellow mariners to perish in the cruel sea, was hideous.'

Curious! I seem to hear a child weeping!
This was the caption to a cartoon in the *Daily Herald*, drawn by the Australian-born cartoonist Will Dyson (1883–1938). It appeared at the conclusion of the Versailles Peace Conference in 1919 and the picture showed the BIG FOUR, President Wilson of the US, Prime Minister Clemenceau of France, President Orlando of Italy and Prime Minister Lloyd George of Britain, leaving the conference hall and hearing a child – signifying the next generation – bewailing the breakdown of their peace efforts. The headline is 'Peace and Future Cannon Fodder'; the caption has 'The Tiger' (Clemenceau) speaking; and the child is prophetically labelled '1940 class'. Dyson did not live to see his prophetic observation come true.

Dad's Army

The long-running BBC TV comedy series *Dad's Army* (1968–77) established in general use a nickname for the Local Defence Volunteers (LDV), formed in Britain at the outbreak of the Second World War and soon renamed officially the HOME GUARD. 'Dad's Army' was a posthumous nickname given by those looking back on the exploits of this civilian force (though its members were uniformed and attached to army units). In other words, there is no evidence that the term was actually used during the war. Many of the members were elderly men.

Daddy, what did YOU do in the Great War?

See WHAT DID YOU DO IN THE GREAT WAR?

Danger UXB [Danger unexploded bomb]

The abbreviation 'UXB' was *probably* used during the Second World War when it was chalked up or painted up to warn people away. In built-up areas, entire blocks might be cordoned off until the bomb had been dealt with. I am not sure whether 'Danger UXB' was ever written up – the familiarity of the phrase stemming more from a 1979 TV drama series about the activities of a bomb–disposal unit in the Second World War and based on the memoirs *Unexploded Bomb* (1972) by Major A.B. Hartley, MBE, Royal Engineers.

(A) date which will live in infamy

'Yesterday, December 7th 1941, a date which will live in

D

infamy, the United States of America was suddenly and deliberately attacked by naval and air forces of the Empire of Japan' – thus President Franklin D. Roosevelt began his address to Congress, the day after the Japanese attack on Pearl Harbor. In the draft it had said, 'a date which will live in *world history*' and '*simultaneously* and deliberately attacked'. With such strokes did he make his speech seeking a declaration of war against Japan more memorable. However, Palmer and Palmer, *Quotations in History* (1976) has '*date that shall* live in infamy' and *IHAT* (also 1976) has 'day *that will* live in infamy' – both wrong.

dawn patrol
An evocative phrase from flying in the First World War but I do not have a citation. This is the earliest: 'The men … who would fly tomorrow's dawn patrol along the invasion coast' – *R.A.F. Journal* (3 October 1942).

(The) day war broke out …
A catchphrase from the Second World War radio monologues of the droll comedian Robb Wilton (1881–1957). They would begin, for example, with some recollection, such as: 'The day war broke out … my missus said to me, "It's up to you … you've got to stop it." I said, "Stop what?" She said, "The war."' Later, when circumstances changed, Wilton's phrase became 'the day *peace* broke out'.

Dear John
Name for a type of letter sent by a woman to a man telling him that she is breaking off their relationship, perhaps

because she has been carrying on with another man in his absence. Its origins are said to lie in US and Canadian armed forces slang of the Second World War, when faithless girls back home had to find a way to admit they were carrying on with or maybe had become pregnant by other men. It subsequently became the name given to a letter informing a man that he had given the woman VD. Known by 1945: ' "Dear John," the letter began. "I have found someone else whom I think the world of. I think the only way out is for us to get a divorce," it said. They usually began like that, those letters that told of infidelity on the part of the wives of servicemen ... The men called them "Dear Johns"' *Democrat & Chronicle* (Rochester, NY) (17 August 1945).

D-Day

Meaning 'an important day when something is due to begin', the most frequent allusion is to 6 June 1944, the day under the code-named Operation Overlord on which the Allies began their landings in northern France in order to push back German forces from occupied France. Like **'H-Hour'**, 'D-Day' is a military way of detailing the stages of an operation. The 'D' just reinforces the 'Day' on which the plan is to be put into effect and enables successive days to be labelled 'D-Day plus one', etc. 'D-Day' and 'H-Hour' are probably of American origin and may first have been used by the American Expeditionary Force at the end of the First World War. 'Field Order No 8' (dated 7 September 1918) stated: 'The First Army will attack at H-Hour on D-Day with the object of forcing the evacuation of St.

D

Mihiel salient.' In British usage, ZERO HOUR was probably the more popular up to this point.

Compare **Der Tag** [The Day], a German phrase from the First World War. Partridge/*Long Trail* has that it meant variously: ' "The day we Germans declare war on England" or "conquer England", or "come into our own". Popularized by [British] journalists and used by officers, often facetiously for any much-desired date or goal.'

6 June 1944 came to be referred to as **'the Longest Day'** (as in the title of a book by Cornelius Ryan, 1959, and the subsequent film, 1962) because Erwin Rommel, the German general, had commented on the prospect of an Allied invasion two months before and had declared: 'The first 24 hours will be decisive … for the Allies as well as Germany it will be the longest day.'

Desert Fox
Nickname of the German Field Marshal Erwin Rommel (1891–1944), noted for his audacious generalship in North Africa during the Second World War. A fox also known as the pale fox does inhabit North Africa, so presumably this is the one that attracted the original sobriquet.

Desert Rats
Nickname of the British 7th Armoured Division, which served throughout the North Africa campaign in the Second World War and adopted the badge of a desert rat (the jerboa). The division made use of 'scurrying and biting' tactics in desert warfare and later fought in the invasion of occupied Europe, from Normandy onwards. 'Dear Desert

Rats, may your glory ever shine' – Winston Churchill, *Victory* (1946).

Dig for victory

Shortage of foodstuffs was an immediate concern in the UK upon the outbreak of the Second World War. On 4 October 1939, Sir Reginald Dorman Smith, the Minister of Agriculture, broadcast these words: 'Half a million more allotments, properly worked, will provide potatoes and vegetables that will feed another million adults and one-and-a-half million children for eight months out of twelve ... So, let's get going. Let "Dig for victory" be the motto of everyone with a garden and of every able-bodied man and woman capable of digging an allotment in their spare time.' A poster bearing the slogan showed a booted foot pushing a spade into the earth. Consequently, the number of allotments rose from 815,000 in 1939 to 1,400,000 in 1943. The American equivalent was the **'Garden for Victory'** campaign and its **'Victory Gardens'**.

dirigible

A steerable balloon or airship – see also ZEPPELIN – as compared to a captive one. The word, known in English since 1550, comes from the Latin *dirigere*, 'to steer'. The application to a balloon was known by 1885 and was thus in place by the time of the First World War. On 28 April 1927, the *Glasgow Herald* reported: 'A new dictionary of air terms has been compiled ... So far as England is concerned, the word "dirigible" will disappear and only "airship" remain' – a prediction that proved correct, except of course that airships barely survived the next decade.

D

displaced person
What a refugee became known as when living in a Displaced Persons' camp. The term was known by 1944 and in the Second World War referred to people removed from their home country by military or political pressure and, for example, non-Germans compelled to work in Germany and thereafter homeless (*OED*).

(to) do one's bit
To make one's contribution to the war effort – an expression popular in the First World War. Known by 1889, it was perhaps used more by people at home than by soldiers on the Front. It was also applied to a man making his contribution by signing up and going away to fight – as in the song 'GOOD-BYE-EE' which begins, 'Brother Bertie went away / To do his bit the other day ...'

dogfight
A battle taking place in the air between two planes, from the end of the First World War and especially in the Second. The word had meant a 'scrap' since the 1880s. 'The battle develops into a "dog-fight", small groups of machines engaging each other in a fight to the death' – A.E. Illingworth, *Fly Papers* (1919).

domestic front
See HOME FRONT.

Don't forget the diver!
See I'M GOING DOWN NOW, SIR!

Don't you know there's a war on?

A reproof aimed at anyone who unreasonably complained about anything – shortages, inconveniences – at the time of the Second World War. Ironically, however, it seems to have been most popular *after* that war was over – and still survives in pockets of memory. The catchphrase was popularized in routines by the British variety act of Hatton and Manners in the 1940s. Will Hatton portrayed a Cockney chappie and Ethel Manners his Lancashire lass. In *The Changing Face of Britain* (1941), the cartoonist 'Fougasse' (Kenneth Bird) reproduces one of his works (first published in *Punch* on 14 February 1940) in which a military person in uniform (just possibly female) is saying down the phone: 'Look here, Major, don't you realise that there's a war on?'

It seems to have spread to the US. James Stewart exclaims 'Don't you know there's a war on?' in the film *It's a Wonderful Life* (1946). From *The Guardian* (6 January 1996): 'My Yorkshire mother, 50 years ago, told me, "Don't pinkle with your food, there's a war on.'

But the necessity for such a catchphrase long preceded this coinage. Partridge/*Long Trail* has the similar **'Remember there's a war on'** dating from the First World War. He glosses it: 'Don't waste time; don't be frivolous; let's get back to our real job.' John Betjeman, in a letter to Cyril Connolly of 19 October 1939 (i.e. within weeks of the outbreak of the Second World War), was writing: 'We must all do our bit. *There's a war on, you know* [his italics].'

doodlebug

A German pilotless flying bomb, Hitler's V-1, aimed at

D

London and other places towards the end of the Second World War; a missile that had a distinctive roar until the motors cut out and the whole craft curved down on to the target; a 'terror' as well as a destructive weapon', like the V-2 rocket that followed. More than 10,000 doodlebugs were launched, each carrying nearly a ton of explosives. 'The first fighter pilot to shoot down what the R.A.F. men call a "doodlebug" was Flight Sergeant Maurice Rose, of Glasgow' – *The Times* (22 June 1944). '*The doodle-bug*. The new weapon with which our enemy has attacked us has borne a number of names since its appearance over Southern England on 13 June ... The public in London has now generally accepted doodle bug, doodle bomb or simply doodle' – *Notes & Queries* (9 September 1944).

DORA

This acronym for the Defence of the Realm Act was personalized by cartoonists as an elderly woman saying 'no' to most things because it laid down restrictions of all kinds for the duration of the First World War. First enacted in 1914, it was repeatedly extended thereafter. For example, it enabled the War Office to censor all cables and foreign correspondence. DORA was also used by Winston Churchill (as Home Secretary) in 1916 to bring the liquor industry, including public houses and breweries, under Government control in certain areas – particularly on the Scottish border where huge munitions factories were located. Pub landlords there became civil servants and were charged with not allowing people to get drunk. 'We are up against official secrets again. A lady called Dora: you will become well acquainted with her' – Ian Hay, *The Last Million* (1918).

doughboy

An American soldier in the First World War. The word had
first been used in the American Civil War. Various
suggestions have been made as to its origin. It may derive
from the name of a 'fried sweet cornmeal cake by 1770, then
a small globular biscuit [compare 'dough-nut'] served to
sailors, then a globular brass button on some Civil War
uniforms, then for soldiers themselves' – *IHAT.*

dreadnought

Name (literally, 'fear nothing') given to the class of British
big-gun destroyers developed in the years prior to the First
World War. *Dreadnought* was the name of the first such
battleship, launched in February 1906. Admiral Lord Fisher
was sufficiently identified with the strategy, which proved
correct in defeating German sea power, that when he was
elevated to the peerage he took as his motto 'Fear God
and Dread Nought'. Presumably it was the sailors on board
such ships who were to dread nought: the enemy was
supposed to dread the battleship. The first destroyer of this
class was so named in 1906 but there had been a tradition in
the British Navy of giving the name *Dreadnought* to
battleships that went back to the reign of Queen Elizabeth I.
A 'dreadnought' was also the name given to a stout outer
garment worn in bad weather (known by 1806).

dud

A bomb that fails to explode. Having previously been applied
to an inefficient person or thing, in the First World War it
was applied especially to an explosive shell that so failed.

D

Dunkirk spirit

National resolve that is said to result from a significant
defeat. The *OED* does not find this phrase until 1956,
though it does find 'to do a Dunkirk' (meaning 'to extract
oneself from disaster') as early as 1944. Both phrases allude
to the evacuation from the northern French town of
Dunkerque/Dunkirk in May/June 1940. Retreating in the
face of the German advance, British and Allied troops had a
remarkable escape in an ad hoc rescue by small boats. About
338,000 were rescued in this way. It was, in anybody's
language, a defeat, but almost at once was seen as some sort
of a triumph. Harold Nicolson wrote to his wife on 31 May:
'It is a magnificent feat once you admit the initial misery of
the thing.' Winston Churchill, in his 'We shall never
surrender' speech to the House of Commons on 4 June,
warned: 'We must be very careful not to assign to this
deliverance the attributes of a victory. Wars are not won by
evacuations. But there was a victory inside this deliverance
which should be noted.' Harold Wilson said in the House of
Commons (26 July 1961): 'I have always deprecated … in
crisis after crisis, appeals to the Dunkirk spirit as an answer
to our problems.' No sooner had he become Prime Minister
than he said in a speech to the Labour Party Conference
(12 December 1964): 'I believe that the spirit of Dunkirk
will once again carry us through to success.'

As for **'the miracle of Dunkirk'**: Basil Liddell Hart, *The
Other Side of the Hill* (1948) has: 'The escape of the British
Army from France has often been called "the miracle of
Dunkirk".' If it has, then it must be because Winston
Churchill said in his 'We shall never surrender speech' of

4 June 1940: 'A miracle of deliverance, achieved by valour, by perseverance, by perfect discipline, by faultless service, by resource, by skill, by unconquerable fidelity, is manifest to us all.'

(for the) duration

Originally, British Army slang of the First World War for the duration of one's enlistment or 'the time during which a war lasts' (which implied 'a very long time indeed', so expressing weariness and frustration). Then it became a short way of referring to 'the duration of the war' or 'until the end of the war'. Often encountered in talk about some restriction on supplies or activities. 'I'm taking up smoking for the duration ...' Noted by 1916. According to Partridge/*Long Trail*, volunteers of 1914–15 enlisted for '"three years or the duration of the war" – an ambiguous phrase'. It soon reappeared during the Second World War. 'We have received a number of letters from country readers offering week-end hospitality for those who must work in London, or "duration" hospitality for their children' – *New Statesman* (19 October 1940). 'The war had intervened ... The Brigadier was pinned down "for the duration"' – Laurence Durrell, *Clea*, Chap. 2 (1960).

Eagle Day

See ADLER TAG.

Eastern Front

In the First World War, this referred to the 1,100-mile (1,770km) Front from Riga on the Baltic to the shores of the Black Sea, where the Germans under Hindenburg and Ludendorf finally defeated the Russians after a series of seesaw battles over Poland (*IHAT*).

Eat greens (for health)

Slogan on posters during the Second World War. On a Hans Schlegel–designed 'Eat greens' poster there was also the legend **'Feed right to feel right'** as a mocked-up headline in *The Daily Telegraph*. There were many of these official exhortations. The Imperial War Museum has a list of ten of them:

1) Make Do and Mend (*q.v.*)
2) Walk Short Distances
3) Save Fuel for Battle
4) Save Kitchen Scraps to Feed the Pigs
5) Don't Waste Water
6) Waste Paper is Still Vital
7) Dig for Victory (*q.v.*)
8) Holiday at Home
9) Eat Greens for Health (as here)
10) Keep Calm and Carry On (*q.v.*)

Eat less bread

A First World War slogan. A poster of around 1917 explained: 'The sinking of foodships by German submarines and the partial failure of the World's wheat crop have brought about a scarcity of wheat and flour which makes it imperative that every household should at once reduce its consumption of BREAD. The Food Controller asks that the weekly consumption of Bread throughout the Country should be reduced by an average of 4 lbs. per head.'

E-boat Alley

The shipping route off the east coast of England during the Second World War – subject to frequent attacks by enemy torpedo boats.

The use of 'E-boat' was current by August 1940 but no one seems quite sure what the 'E' stands for, except as an abbreviation for 'enemy torpedo boat'.

OED rules: 'The view, frequently expressed, that *E* represents German *Eile* "speed" is purely speculative. The usual German word for a speedboat is *Schnellboot*.'

Ein Volk, ein Reich, ein Führer [One people, one realm, one leader]

Nazi slogan first used in September 1940, at the Nuremberg Rally that year.

Compare the slogan subsequently used by the National Party in South Africa's 1948 general election: 'Eie volk, eie taal, eie land [Our own people, our own language, our own land]'.

(at the) eleventh hour of the eleventh day of the eleventh month

This expression was used with resonance at the end of the First World War.

The Armistice that brought hostilities to an end was signed at 5 a.m. on 11 November 1918 and came into force at 11 a.m. that day – 'at the eleventh hour of the eleventh day of the eleventh month'.

emergency rations

Known by 1898 but came to prominence in the First World War. 'A tin of bully-beef, with packets of tea, sugar and biscuits, carried by every infantryman and officially not to be touched except in emergencies and under special orders' – Partridge/*Long Trail*.

Also called **iron rations** (known by 1876), again with the emphasis on their being tinned.

Enemy ears are listening

See WALLS HAVE EARS.

England expects that every man will do his duty and join the Army today

A recruiting slogan towards the end of the First World War. An obvious extension of Horatio Nelson's famous signal to his fleet before the Battle of Trafalgar on 21 October 1805: 'England expects that every man will do his duty'.

At about the same time (1914–18), H.L. Mencken noted a saying in the US: 'England expects every American to do his duty'.

Enlist today

Army recruitment phrase during the First World War. A poster addressed to those employing male servants, read: 'Have you a Butler, Groom, Chauffeur, Gardener or Gamekeeper serving *you* who at this moment should be serving your King and Country? … Have you a man digging your garden who should be digging trenches?' It concluded: 'Ask your men to enlist TO-DAY.'

ENSA

Acronym of the Entertainments National Service Association, an organization of units of entertainers established within two weeks of war being declared in 1939. They toured the 'theatres of war' with their shows. As their standards were somewhat of a concert-party nature, the acronym was also translated as, 'Every Night Something Awful/Atrocious' and 'Even NAAFI Stands Aghast'.

(the) fall of France

Paris fell to the Germans on 14 June 1940 and this significant event was later much referred to by historians as 'the fall of France', sometimes with capital letters. Later in the war, Winston Churchill used the phrase on occasions but I do not think he is really responsible for coining or popularizing it. Indeed, *Life* magazine was already using the phrase (though without capitals) in its issue of 1 July 1940. Churchill did, however, subsequently use the phrase for the title of 'Book 1' and a chapter in the second volume of his *History of the Second World War*.

(a) faraway country of which we know little

In fact what Prime Minister Neville Chamberlain said about Czechoslovakia in a radio broadcast (27 September 1938) was: 'How terrible, fantastic, incredible it is that we should be digging trenches and trying on gas-masks here because of a quarrel in a faraway country between people of whom we know nothing.' But either way, it was an unforgivable thing to have said. An unverified suggestion has been made that he had been anticipated in this kind of short-sighted view of foreign affairs by Sir John Simon, as Foreign Secretary, in a House of Commons speech referring to the Japanese invasion of Manchuria in 1931.

(the) Few

Winston Churchill's classic tribute to the RAF fighter pilots who won the Battle of Britain was in fact made well before the battle had reached its peak or indeed before victory was assured. Speaking in the House of Commons (20 August 1940), he said: 'Never in the field of human conflict was so much owed by so many to so few.' There is a clear echo of Shakespeare's lines 'We few, we happy few, we band of brothers'. In *Henry V*. In *Benham's Book of Quotations* (1948), Sir John Moore (1761–1809) is quoted as saying after the fall of Calpi (where Nelson lost an eye): 'Never was so much work done by so few men.'

Another pre-echo may be found in Vol. 2 of Churchill's own *A History of the English-Speaking Peoples* (1956, but largely written pre-war). In describing a Scottish incursion in 1640 during the run-up to the English Civil War, he writes: 'All the Scots cannon fired and all the English army fled. A contemporary wrote that "Never so many ran from so few with less ado". The English soldiers explained volubly that their flight was not due to fear of the Scots, but to their own discontents.'

Earlier outings of the phraseology in Churchill's own speeches include: 'Never before were there so many people in England and never before have they had so much to eat' (Oldham by-election, 1899); and 'Nowhere else in the world could so enormous a mass of water be held up by so little masonry' (of a Nile dam, 1908).

The bookish phrase 'in the field of human conflict' has tended to be dropped when Churchill's speech is quoted. It is interesting that Harold Nicolson, noting it in his diary, slightly misquotes the passage: '[Winston] says, in referring to the RAF, "never in the history of human conflict *has* so much been owed by so many to so few".' Much later,

Terry Major-Ball was one of those who repeated the first of these errors in *Major Major: Memories of an Older Brother* (1994): 'Never in the history of human conflict has a private soldier been so relieved,' he writes.

The immediate impact of Churchill's phrase was unquestionable, however, and is evidenced by a letter to him of 10 September from Lady Violet Bonham Carter (from the Churchill papers, quoted by Martin Gilbert in Vol. 6 of the official biography): 'Your sentence about the Air-war – "Never in the history [*sic*] of human conflict has [*sic*] so much been owed by so many to so few" – will live as long as words are spoken and remembered. Nothing so simple, so majestic & so true has been said in so great a moment of human history. You have beaten your old enemies "the Classics" into a cocked hat! Even my Father [H.H. Asquith] would have admitted that. How *he* would have loved it!' By 22 September, Churchill's daughter, Mary, was uttering a bon mot in his hearing about the collapse of France through weak leadership: 'Never before has so much been betrayed for so many by so few' – recorded by John Colville, *The Fringes of Power*, Vol. 1 (1985).

fifth column

A group of traitors or infiltrators. Although this expression was much used in the Second World War, its precise origin lay just before in the Spanish Civil War. In October 1936, the Nationalist General Emilio Mola was besieging the Republican-held city of Madrid with four columns. He was asked in a broadcast whether this was sufficient to capture the city and he replied that he was relying on the support of

F

the *quinta columna* [the fifth column], which was already hiding inside the city and which sympathized with his side. *The Fifth Column* was the title of Ernest Hemingway's only play (1938). Some doubt has been cast on the ascription to Mola. Lance Haward (1996) noted that in the *Daily Express* of 27 October 1936, Moscow Radio was quoted as having attributed the phrase to General Franco. In the *Daily Mail* of 7 November, the Guardia Civile in Madrid, disaffected from the Republican cause, was being referred to as 'General Franco's now famous "Fifth Column"'. In Hugh Thomas, *The Spanish Civil War* (1961), it is reported that the expression has been found in *Mundo Obrero* (3 October 1936) and that Lord St Oswald had used the term several weeks earlier in a report to *The Daily Telegraph*.

Fifty million Frenchmen can't be wrong

A good deal of confusion surrounds this saying. As a slightly grudging expression it appears to have originated with American servicemen during the First World War, ironically justifying support for their French allies. The precise number of millions is variable. Partridge/*Catch Phrases* suggests that it was the last line of a First World War song 'extolling the supreme virtue of copulation, though in veiled terms'. Partridge may, however, have been referring to a song with the title (by Rose, Raskin and Fisher), which was not recorded by Sophie Tucker until 15 April 1927. Cole Porter's musical with the title *Fifty Million Frenchmen* opened in New York on 27 November 1929. An unrelated US film with this three-word title was released in 1931.

Where the confusion has crept in is that Texas Guinan (1884–1933), an American nightclub hostess, was refused entry into France with her showgirls in 1931 and said: 'It goes to show that fifty million Frenchmen *can* be wrong.' She returned to America and renamed her show *Too Hot for Paris*. Perversely, the *Oxford Dictionary of Quotations* (1979, 1992) has her saying 'Fifty million Frenchmen *can't* be wrong' in the *New York World-Telegram* on 21 March 1931, and seems to be arguing that she originated the phrase as she had been using it 'six or seven years earlier'. Sometimes it is quoted as '*Forty* million Frenchmen …'

Bernard Shaw also held out against the phrase. He insisted: 'Fifty million Frenchmen can't be right.'

fighter (plane)
This term for a military aircraft designed for aerial combat arose in the First World War – by 1917.

(The) first casualty when war comes is truth
From a speech to the US Senate (in about 1917) by Hiram Johnson, an American all-party senator (1866–1945) – at least, this is according to Burton Stevenson's *Home Book of Quotations* (1948), but the remark remains untraced. It was also quoted in Albert Johnson, *Common English Quotations* (1963). Aeschylus has been mentioned as a possible forerunner. Curiously, yet another Johnson – Samuel – said much the same thing less pithily in *The Idler*, No 30 (11 November 1758): 'Among the calamities of war, may be justly numbered the diminution of the love of truth, by the falsehoods which interest dictates and credulity encourages.' At the time of

the First World War, Arthur (later Lord) Ponsonby used 'When war is declared, Truth is the first casualty' (unattributed) as the motto of his book *Falsehood in Wartime* (1928). Hence, whatever the source, *The First Casualty*, title of a book on propaganda in wartime (1975) by Phillip Knightley.

Final Solution [Endlösung] (of the Jewish Problem)

A euphemistic term used by Nazi officials from the summer of 1941 onwards when referring to Adolf Hitler's plan to exterminate the Jews of Europe. A directive (drafted by Adolf Eichmann) was sent by Hermann Goering to Reinhard Heydrich on 31 July 1941: 'Submit to me as soon as possible a draft showing … measures already taken for the execution of the intended final solution of the Jewish question.' Gerald Reitlinger, in his book *The Final Solution* (1953), says that the choice of phrase was probably, though not certainly, Hitler's own. Before then it had been used in a non-specific way to cover other possibilities, such as emigration. It is estimated that the 'final solution' led to the deaths of up to six million Jews.

flame thrower

Translation of *Flammenwerfer*, a weapon first used by the Germans at the Battle of Verdun (21 February 1916), the term known by 1917. It was originally called a 'flame projector' by the British.

fog of war

The confusion of events amid the smoke of battle. In 1938, the British military historian Basil Liddell Hart wrote a book entitled *Through the Fog of War* – a potted history of the First World War to see what lessons could be learned from it 'under the shadow of another "Great War"' – but he does not explain the relevance or provenance of the title.

'The duty of writing from time to time these appreciations, and making forecasts on necessarily imperfect information, is a difficult task. It demands sound knowledge of military service, a trained judgment, assiduous study, and a natural gift for piercing the fog of war' – 'The Literature of the Russo-Japanese War' by a 'British Officer' in *The American Historical Review* (July 1911). So, wherever it came from, it seems to have been an established phrase before the First World War.

Perhaps one should conclude that the phrase arose through 19th-century 'war studies' under the influence of Karl Von Clausewitz and based on an image he used in *Vom Kriege* (1832): 'All action must be planned in a mere twilight, which – like the effect of a fog or moonshine – gives to things exaggerated dimension and an unnatural appearance.' However, neither the phrase *Nebel des Krieg(e)s* (fog of war) nor anything like it actually appears in his work. So quite how the phrase caught on is not yet apparent.

For king and country

The alliterative linking of the two words 'king' and 'country' is of long standing. Francis Bacon (1625) wrote: 'Be so true to thyselfe, as thou be not false to others; specially to thy King, and Country.' Earlier, Shakespeare, *Henry VI, Part 2*, I.iii.157 (1597) has: 'But God in mercy so deal with my soul / As I in duty love my king and country!'

Here, however, it is a reduction of the First World War recruiting slogan 'Your King and Country Need You'. In that war, 'For king and country' was the official answer to the question: 'What are we fighting for?'

(the) Forces' Sweetheart

Vera Lynn (b. 1917 – and made a Dame of the British Empire in 1975) – popular singer who entertained servicemen throughout the Second World War in concerts and on radio. Her distinctive contralto voice still evokes the period instantly – particularly when songs such as '(THE) WHITE CLIFFS OF DOVER' and 'WE'LL MEET AGAIN' are revived. And reduces grown men to tears.

Forgotten Army

Nickname given to the British Army in India and South-East Asia, and more precisely, in Burma and Malaya during the Second World War. According to John Connell in his book *Auchinleck* (1959), it was mentioned in a despatch by Stuart Emeny, a *News Chronicle* war correspondent, in the summer of 1943, but the idea behind it had long been current with the soldiers. The name may have been coined by Lieutenant General Sir William Slim, who is said to have remarked to his men: 'When you go home don't worry about what to tell your loved ones and friends about service in Asia. No one will know where you were, or where it is if you do. You are, and will remain "The Forgotten Army".'

Similarly, when he took command, Lord Louis Mountbatten is reported to have told his troops: 'Well, let me tell you that this is not the Forgotten Front, and you are not the Forgotten Army. In fact, nobody has even heard of you.'

Former Naval Person
Code name of Winston Churchill as Prime Minister in his cables to President Roosevelt during the Second World War. He had previously been referred to as 'Naval Person' when he had held the office of First Lord of the Admiralty at the outbreak of war.

For you, Tommy, the war is over!
Said by a German capturing a British soldier during the Second World War (TOMMY being the traditional nickname for such), but few citations are to hand. Partridge/*Catch Phrases* has it as said, rather, by Italians to British prisoners of war in 1940–5 and without the 'Tommy'.

A correspondent (1995), stated: 'Among the thousands of prisoners I met there was none who had not been greeted with this phrase on his entrance into captivity.'

Sam Kydd, the British film character actor, entitled his war memoirs *For You the War Is Over* (1974) and described his own capture by the Germans at Calais in May 1940 after he had only been six days on active service: '[The officer] sported a monocle and with the effort of keeping it in place his face assumed a twisted grin just like Erich Von Stroheim. He announced the immortal words, "For you ze VOR is OVair!"'

It was used again as a book title in 1983 by the Hon. Philip Kindersley, who was captured at Tunis at Christmas in 1942. Both are pre-dated by Jan Gerstel's *The War for You*

Is Over (1960). It has also been suggested that it might have been what a doctor or nurse would have said to a British soldier wounded in the First World War and before being returned to 'Blighty' for treatment.

The journalist James Cameron reportedly once described how he was captured in North Africa during the Second World War and was told by none other than Rommel that 'For you the war is over'.

For your tomorrow we gave our today

By the time of the Second World War it was frequently stated that these 'words are a translation from the Greek'. Famously, this version appeared on the 2nd British Division's memorial at Kohima War Cemetery, Assam (now Nagaland), in India (and on many other war graves round the world):

> When you go home
> Tell them of us and say
> For your tomorrow
> We gave our today.

Many people still appear to think that it is an allusion to the Greek poet Simonides – but, as with WENT THE DAY WELL? – this is the work of the English poet and academic, J.M. Edmonds (1875–1958), originally:

> When you go home, tell them of us and say,
> 'For your tomorrow these gave their today.'

This is 'for a British graveyard in France', another

suggested epitaph by Edmonds which appeared in *The Times Literary Supplement* (4 July 1918). The second line of Edmonds's original should not read 'For your tomorrows', as in the *Oxford Dictionary of Quotations* (1992).

The verse appears as epigraph to the 1959 film *Yesterday's Enemy* about the Burma campaign – and, apparently, inspired the title.

The BBC received a somewhat crusty letter from Edmonds (by this time a Fellow of Jesus College, Cambridge), dated 23 July 1953, in which he said, 'I thought the Greek origin of my epitaph used – and altered – at Kohima had been denied in print often enough; but here it is again. It is no translation, nor is it true to say it was suggested by one of the beautiful couplets which you will find in *Lyrica Graeca* (Loeb Classical Library), though I *was* at work on that book in 1917 when my Twelve War Epitaphs were first printed in *The Times* and its *Literary Supplement* ... The epitaph, of course, should be used only abroad. Used in England its "home" may be just round the corner – which makes the whole thing laughable.'

Fourteen Points

President Wilson's Fourteen Points, set out in an address to Congress (8 January 1918), were the US's demands for a new world order following the First World War. They included proposals for 'open covenants of peace, openly arrived at', freedom of the seas, free trade and disarmament. Georges Clemenceau, the French Prime Minister, commented at the Versailles Peace Conference, 'The good Lord has only ten.'

(We are) Fred Karno's army

Line from an anonymous song popular in the trenches of the First World War. It was sung to the tune of the hymn 'The Church's One Foundation':

> We are Fred Karno's army, the ragtime infantry.
> We cannot fight, we cannot shoot, what bleeding use
>   are we?
> And when we get to Berlin we'll hear the Kaiser say,
> 'Hoch, hoch! Mein Gott, what a bloody rotten lot, are
>   the ragtime infantry.'

'Fred Karno', used adjectivally to mean 'inept, disorganized', was applied humorously to the new British Army raised to fight in the First World War. The name came from the leader – actually, Fred Westcott (d. 1941) – of a music-hall comedy troupe that was popular in the early years of the twentieth century. Hence: 'Fred Karno's army', 'Fred Karno outfit', etc.

Freedom is in peril – defend it with all your might

Slogan on a morale-building poster, issued in 1939. It was selected by George Orwell at the end of the Second World War as an example of a 'futile slogan obviously incapable of stirring strong feelings or being circulated by word of mouth … One has to take into account the fact that nearly all English people dislike anything that sounds high-flown or boastful. Slogans like "They Shall Not Pass", or "Better To Die On Your Feet Than Live On Your Knees", which have thrilled continental nations, seem slightly embarrassing to an Englishman, especially a working man.' To which Angus Calder added in *The People's War* (1969): 'It was partly from the de-sensitized prose of most of the British press during the war, from the desertion of subtleties of meaning in favour of slogans, that George Orwell derived the notion of Newspeak, the vocabulary of totalitarianism' in *Nineteen Eighty-Four*.

(the) Front
The foremost battle line, a term used since the mid-17th century but particularly during the First World War and often with a capital 'F'. See also under EASTERN − / HOME − / SECOND − / WESTERN −. Enabled a joke of G.K. Chesterton's: during the First World War, a patriotic hostess pointedly asked the more than portly writer, 'Why are you not out at the Front?' He replied to her, gently: 'Madam, if you go round to the side, you will find that I am' − quoted in A.N. Wilson, *Hilaire Belloc* (1984).

(der) Führer [the leader]
Part of the title *Führer und Reichskanzler* taken by Adolf Hitler when, in 1934, he united the roles of Chancellor and President. It imitated the title already taken by the Italian dictator, Benito Mussolini: *Il Duce*.

(the) full monty
This phrase meaning, 'the full amount, everything included' became suddenly popular in British English in the early 1990s but had been current since the early 1980s. Many are the explanations that have been advanced for it but one

possibly links it back to the Second World War, if it had something to do with being dressed in a full complement of jacket, trousers, waistcoat and overcoat from the tailors Montague Burton (first established in Chesterfield in 1904 and later to become Burton Menswear). A correspondent wrote (1996): 'When I started work in insurance in Manchester in 1949, the full monty was a three-piece suit [from Montague Burton] – de rigueur in those circles – [which you could get] for the price of a two-piece at the opposition – the "fifty shilling" tailor, later John Collier.' In fact, the most popular presumed origin for the phrase has something to do with Sir Montague Burton (1885–1952), founder of Burton menswear stores, and his supplying of a full suit and accessories to purchasers, especially those being demobilized from the forces. As the *Dictionary of National Biography* records, a quarter of all uniforms provided in this country in the 1939–45 war were made by 'Monty' Burton's company, as were a third of the clothes issued on demob. But if 'full monty' had anything to do with Montague Burton or demobbed servicemen's clothes, it is surprising that Eric Partridge and his reviser Paul Beale had never heard of it.

gas mask/respirator

A necessary protective device after the Germans first used gas against French and British forces at the Second Battle of Ypres in April 1915. Earlier that year they had used chlorine gas against the Russians on the Eastern Front. The Hague Conference of 1907 had expressly forbidden use of poison gases in warfare. Gas masks were much in evidence at the start of the Second World War – when thought to be a vital accessory for all civilians – but were never used.

(the) gathering storm

The title of Vol. 1 of Winston Churchill's history of *The Second World War*, published in 1948, was *The Gathering Storm*. This phrase had acquired much resonance during the 1930s and, after the Second World War, it became a cliché of documentaries about the war's approach, often in the form **'Storm clouds were gathering over Europe'**.

It has been suggested that Churchill took this title from H.G. Wells, *The War of the Worlds* (1898). The phrase is used straightforwardly in chapter 10 and is also used in a quasi-metaphorical way to describe some flickering in the sky in chapter 13, which might tell of approaching Martians. There is no question that Churchill read Wells, admired him and told him so, but he does not seem to have used the phrase at all in the interim, while lots of other people did. For example, it had already been used about the approach of war by Anthony Eden in a speech to the National Association of Manufacturers in New York in 1938. Then

G

William Empson entitled a book of poems *The Gathering Storm* in 1940 (of all years).

Indeed, the metaphorical use with regard to political storms and crises goes well back. Working backwards – and of obvious relevance to the approach of the Second World War – in 1929, *Slings and Arrows: Sayings Chosen from the Speeches of the Rt. Hon. David Lloyd George*, included the words: 'Storm clouds are gathering over Europe. It will need all the wisdom, all the calm, all the judgement of the mariners who are guiding the ship.' Additionally, in August 1911, Lloyd George had written to Churchill: 'The thunderclouds are gathering. I am not at all satisfied that we are prepared, or that we are preparing.'

More general uses of the phrase, still working backwards, are: in Trotsky's *My Life*, chapter 19 (1930) and referring to the period of the Russian Revolution and the First World War, he wrote: 'In the meantime, clouds were gathering overhead, and during 1916 they grew very dark'; 'Wherever we look dark storm-clouds are gathering thickly round the monarchy' – *The Living Age* (20 March 1889); 'On his release, in 1780, Linguet went abroad again, and once more plunged into newspaper war. Storm clouds were gathering ominously then, and every shot fired by the spleenful writer against the tottering upholders of misrule told heavily. For all this, when the Revolution actually broke out, Linguet declared himself against it' – *The Living Age* (14 March 1874); 'Thus in the beginning of November, 1837, joy reigned in Algiers, and the future was forgotten – while the storm clouds were gathering over the Colony, which burst with a suddenness and fury as terrible as unexpected' – John

Watts de Peyster, 'Personal and Military History of Philip Kearny, Major-General United States Volunteers' (1869); an anonymous poet of the 1840s wrote in *Punch*: 'Storm-clouds were over Europe, light slept on England's breast. / The nation's heaved with earthquake throes, but / A cry went up from Passaro unto the Baltic shore, / And every tongue but England's had its echo in the roar.' And ages before all this, Robert Burns wrote in 'Tam o'Shanter' (1791) of: 'Our hame, / Where sits our sulky sullen dame, / Gathering her brows like gathering storm / Nursing her wrath to keep it warm.'

If we are still looking for a trigger to Churchill's use of the phrase, here is another intriguing suggestion. Irving Berlin wrote 'God Bless America' in 1918 but put it on ice for twenty years – so the 1938 version (a rewrite) was in fact its first publication. And in 1938, storm clouds were gathering over Europe very much indeed. The introduction he wrote then was intended to be spoken before the song:

> While the storm clouds gather far across the sea,
> Let us swear allegiance to a land that's free,
> Let us all be grateful for a land so fair,
> As we raise our voices in a solemn prayer …

The Music Division of the Library of Congress points out that this introductory stanza 'since forgotten, despite the popularity of the song's refrain', does not appear in either the original lead sheet for the song, nor in the original version of the song's lyrics in Berlin's hand, nor in a copy made for President Eisenhower (all held in the Library's Berlin Collection).

G

Whatever the case, we are now presented with the amusing possibility that when Irving Berlin was invited to have lunch with Churchill at Downing Street in 1944 – when *Isaiah* Berlin had been intended – they might have had something to talk about after all. As it was, Churchill was puzzled by the fact that Mr Berlin, the composer, had nothing brilliant to say about American politics as Mr Berlin, the philosopher/diplomat, had been expected to do. As to the post-Second World War cliché, it was obviously encouraged by Churchill's title. It was certainly established as a cliché by 1967 when it was used in a wartime parody by the BBC radio show *Round the Horne*. It was still going strong in Ian Kershaw's 1998 biography, *Hitler 1889–1936: Hubris*, as 'The storm-clouds were gathering over Europe.'

Germany calling, Germany calling!

William Joyce, an Irish-American (1906–46) who broadcast Nazi propaganda from Hamburg during the Second World War, was found guilty of treason (on the technicality that he held a British passport at the beginning of the war) and was hanged in 1946. He had a threatening, sneering, lower-middle-class delivery, which made his call-sign sound more like 'Jarmany calling'. Although Joyce was treated mostly as a joke in wartime Britain, he is credited with giving rise to some unsettling rumours. No one seemed to have heard the particular broadcast in question, but it got about that he had said the clock on Darlington Town Hall was two minutes slow, and so it was supposed to be.

His nickname of **'Lord Haw-Haw'** was inappropriate, as he did not sound the slightest bit aristocratic. *That* soubriquet had been applied by Jonah Barrington, the *Daily Express* radio correspondent, to Joyce's predecessor who *did* speak with a cultured accent but lasted only a few weeks from September 1939. This original was Norman Baillie-Stewart. He is said to have sounded like Claud Hulbert or one of the Western Brothers. An imaginary drawing appeared in the *Daily Express* of a Bertie Woosterish character with a monocle and receding chin. In one broadcast, Baillie-Stewart said that he understood there was a popular English song called 'We're Going to Hang Out the Washing on the Siegfried Line' which ended 'If the Siegfried Line's still there'. 'Curiously enoff,' he said, 'the Siegfried Line is still they-ah.'

Geronimo!

It was during the North African campaign of November 1942 that US paratroopers are said first to have shouted 'Geronimo!' as they jumped out of planes. It then became customary to do so and turned into a popular exclamation akin to 'Eureka!' A number of Native Americans in the paratroop units coined and popularized the expression, recalling the actual Apache Geronimo, who died in 1909. It is said that when Geronimo was being pursued by the army over some steep hills near Fort Sill, Oklahoma, he made a leap on horseback over a sheer cliff into water. As the troops did not dare follow him, he cried 'Geronimo!' as he leapt. Some of the paratroopers who were trained at Fort Bragg and Fort Campbell adopted this shout, not least because it reminded them to breathe deeply during a jump. In 1939, there had been a film entitled *Geronimo*, which may have reminded them. 'A defiant yell, "Geronimo!" echoed over North Africa last week' – *Newsweek* (30 November 1942).

(to) get it
To be killed – British Army slang, from the First World War.

GIs
A self-imposed nickname for the American serviceman, much of whose supplies were marked with these initials. They are said to have stood for 'Government Issue', 'Garrison Issue', 'General Issue' or even 'Galvanized Iron'. There are many explanations. But the initials seemed appropriate to the men themselves. Their allies in the Second World War seized on the description. **GI Joe** became the name for any American soldier, from June 1942, 'Joe' having become the popular name for any typical guy by then.

Go to hell, Babe Ruth – American, you die!
George Herman Ruth (1895–1948), the US professional baseball player, was the most popular baseball player in the history of the game. He was so famous that a battle cry of Japanese soldiers first heard in the Pacific in 1942 was: 'Go to hell, Babe Ruth – American, you die.'

Go to it!
Slogan for a voluntary labour force in wartime. In the summer of 1940, the Minister of Supply, Herbert Morrison, called for such a force in words that echoed the public mood after Dunkirk. The slogan was used in a campaign run by the S.H. Benson agency (which later indulged in self-parody

on behalf of Bovril, with 'Glow to it' in 1951–2). 'Go to it', meaning 'to act vigorously, set to with a will' dates at least from the early 19th century. In Shakespeare, it means something else, of course: 'Die for adultery! No: / The wren goes to't, and the small gilded fly / Does lecher in my sight' – *King Lear*, IV.vi.112 (1605). See also OLD BILL.

gone for a burton

Early in the Second World War – by 1941 – an RAF expression arose to describe what had happened to a missing person, presumed dead. He had 'gone for a burton', meaning that he had gone for a drink (*in* the drink = the sea) or, as another phrase put it, 'he'd bought it'. Folk memory has it that during the 1930s 'gone for a Burton' had been used in advertisements to promote a Bass beer known in the trade as 'a Burton' (though, in fact, several ales are produced at Burton-on-Trent). More positive proof is lacking. Other fanciful theories are that RAF casualty records were kept in an office above or near a branch of Burton Menswear in Blackpool, and that Morse Code instruction for wireless operators/air gunners took place in a converted billiards hall above Burton's in the same town (and failure in tests meant posting off the course – a fairly minor kind of 'death'). Probably no more than a coincidental use of the name Burton, and there are numerous other explanations for this involving other Burtons.

(to have a) good war

To survive and have experiences which, though testing, add to a person's achievements. Probably first used in relation to combatants in the Second World War. Lord Moran in *Churchill: The Struggle for Survival* made a 1943 allusion: 'But it was [Lord] Wavell who said to me, "I have had a bad war".' In Henry Reed's radio play of 1959, *Not a Drum Was Heard: the War Memoirs of General Gland*, Gland says: 'It was, I think a *good* war, one of the best there have so far been. I've often advanced the view that it was a war deserving of better generalship than it received on either side.'

Usually, however, it is a good war in the sense of a personally successful or enjoyable one that is being talked about. Latterly, uses have been mostly figurative. In his *European Diary*, Roy Jenkins has this entry for 19 February 1979: 'Bill Rodgers ... clearly thought he had had, as Peter Jenkins put it, "a good war" during the strike period and was exhilarated by having made a public breakthrough.' From Julian Critchley MP in *The Guardian* (3 May 1989): 'I well remember some years ago at the Savoy a colleague who had had a good war leaping to his feet (before the Loyal Toast) in order to pull back the curtains which separated the party from the outside world ...' From *The Independent* (13 July 1989): 'British Rail has not had a good war. The public relations battle in the industrial dispute seems to have been all but lost.' 'He had what the men call a good war; we'd call it a bad war I dare say, a lot of killing and fighting' – P.D. James, *An Unsuitable Job for a Woman*, chapter 4 (1972).

Good-bye-ee!

A usage that appears to have originated with the First World War song, 'Goodbye-ee', written by R.P. Weston and Bert Lee in 1915. The chorus goes:

Good-bye-ee, good-bye-ee!
Wipe the tear, baby dear, from your eye-ee,
Tho' it's hard to part, I know,
I'll be tickled to death to go.
Don't cry-ee! Don't sigh-ee,
There's a silver lining in the sky-ee.
Bonsoir, old thing! Cheer-i-o, chin chin!
Nah poo! Toodle-oo! Good-bye-ee!

'Nah poo' or **'Napoo'** is derived from the French *il n'y en a plus* [there is no more] and came to be used as an all-purpose expression for whatever is gone, finished – a disappointing state of affairs. Partridge/*Long Trail* comments: 'Ostensibly it was skit, a parody, a satire on home-sick and leave-taking songs, but often the melancholy it was intended to whip out of existence would creep quietly back into the singing voices.' It may have originated with the French shopkeeper's stock reply when asked for something that had sold out.

Goodbye to all that
Phrase popularized by Robert Graves in the title of his autobiographical volume *Goodbye To All That* (1929) – a farewell to his participation in the First World War and to an unhappy period in his private life.

goose step
A marching step in which the legs are alternately raised forward, straight out without bending the knees. Used by various armies but principally associated with the Prussian

military – from the early 19th century right through to the German Army of the Second World War. Perhaps this method is somewhat reminiscent of the way a goose, with its short legs and webbed feet, seems to strut.

Gott strafe England [God punish England]

A German propaganda slogan and indeed common salutation from the First World War. It apparently originated, or at least made an early appearance, in a book called *Schwert und Myrte* (1914) by Alfred Funke. Mocked in *Punch* (12 May 1915). 'The recognised toast throughout Hunland', according to the *Daily Mirror* (1 November 1916). It led to the verb 'to strafe', meaning to attack, preferably in a sweeping manner as from a low-flying aircraft, but applied to anything. 'I never saw a billet like this for flies … We are trying poison too, but however we may "strafe" there are just as many left' – A.D. Gillespie, *Letters from Flanders* (1916). 'The Germans are called the Gott-strafers, and strafe is becoming a comic English word' – *The Times Literary Supplement* (10 February 1916).

Green Goddess

Alliterative nickname applied to a type of Second World War fire engine that was indeed painted green. Perhaps the first application had been to a British steam locomotive in the 1920s. Subsequently, the name has been given to a type of Liverpool tram, a crème de menthe cocktail, a lettuce salad, a lily, and so on. Perhaps all these uses derive from William Archer's play entitled *The Green Goddess* (1921; films US 1923 and 1930).

gremlin

This name for a kind of imp or sprite said to get into aircraft and other machinery and make it malfunction was popular in the RAF during the Second World War, although it may have originated during the First.

The name first appeared in print in 1929, and seems to have been derived from 'goblin', possibly blended with 'Fremlin's' (the name of a Kent beer).

'As he flew round, he wished that his instructor had never told him about the Little People, a mythological bunch of good and bad fairies originally invented by the Royal Naval Air Service in the Great War ... Those awful little people, the Gremlins, who run up and down the wing with scissors going "snip, snap, snip" made him sweat' – Charles Graves, *The Thin Blue Line, or Adventures in the RAF* (1941).

Roald Dahl wrote a children's book called *The Gremlins* as early as 1943, which undoubtedly also helped to popularize the term.

guinea pigs

RAF pilots from the Second World War who had suffered burns and were treated at the Queen Victoria Hospital, East Grinstead, under the noted plastic surgeon Sir Archibald McIndoe. A Guinea Pig Club was set up to take care of their welfare for as long as there were survivors. It was headed by a Chief Guinea Pig – first of all McIndoe, and then Group Captain Tom Gleave. The name 'guinea pig' in this instance came from the patients feeling they were being experimented on to develop new techniques of surgery.

guilty men

Guilty Men was the title of a tract, published in July 1940, 'which may rank as literature' (A.J.P. Taylor). It was written by Michael Foot, Frank Owen and Peter Howard using the pseudonym 'Cato' and it taunted the proponents of APPEASEMENT who had brought about the situation whereby Britain had had to go to war with Germany. The preface contains this anecdote: 'On a spring day in 1793 a crowd of angry men burst their way through the doors of the assembly room where the French Convention was in session. A discomforted figure addressed them from the rostrum. "What do the people desire?" he asked. "The Convention has only their welfare at heart." The leader of the angry crowd replied, "The people haven't come here to be given a lot of phrases. They demand a dozen guilty men."' The phrase 'We name the guilty men' subsequently became a cliché of popular 'investigative' journalism.

gung-ho

Meaning 'enthusiastic, fiery' – if somewhat carelessly so – the phrase derives from Chinese *kung* plus *ho* meaning 'work together' or *keng ho*, meaning 'more fiery'. It became a semi-official slogan of the US Marines during the Second World War by 1942 – and is said to have been chosen by Lieut. Gen. Evans F. Carlson. Hence, in 1943, a film about the Marines had the title *Gung Ho!* In Geoff Chapple, *Rewi Alley of China* (1980), it is stated that the phrase was coined in 1938 and used as the motto of the Chinese Industrial Cooperatives Association.

guns before butter

When a nation is under pressure to choose between material comforts and some kind of war effort, the choice has to be made between 'guns *and* butter'. Some will urge 'guns *before* butter'. 'We can do without butter, but, despite all our love of peace, not without arms. One cannot shoot with butter, but with guns' from the translation of a speech by Joseph Goebbels given in Berlin (17 January 1936). Later that same year, Hermann Goering said in a broadcast, 'Guns will make us powerful; butter will only make us fat,' so he may also be credited with the 'guns or butter' slogan. But there is a third candidate. Airey Neave, in his book *Nuremberg* (1978), stated of Rudolf Hess: 'It was he who urged the German people to make sacrifices and coined the phrase: "Guns before butter".'

'(We're Going to) Hang out the Washing on the Siegfried Line'

This was a popular song written by Ulster songwriter Jimmy Kennedy while he was a Captain in the British Expeditionary Force during the early stages of the Second World War. The Siegfried Line was originally the line of fortifications occupied by the Germans in France during the First World War. This was their name for it – the British called it the Hindenburg Line. In the run-up to the Second World War, the name was given to a line of defence constructed by the Germans along their western frontier. (The French meanwhile constructed the Maginot Line to keep the Germans out, but this was ineffective because they invaded through Belgium.) The song was used as a morale-booster during the war, particularly up to the fall of France.

> We're going to hang out the washing on the
>   Siegfried Line.
> Have you any dirty washing, mother dear?
> We're gonna hang out the washing on the
>   Siegfried Line.
> 'Cause the washing day is here.

'What song is to be the "Tipperary" of this war? The first candidate would seem to be "The Washing on the Siegfried Line". Its chorus is sufficiently simple and singable' – *The Times* (22 September 1939).

Hang the Kaiser!

Given the role played in the First World War by Kaiser
Wilhelm II, there was pressure for retribution at the war's
end during the 1918 British General Election. The demand
was largely fuelled by the press and this slogan became
current. The Treaty of Versailles (1919) committed the
Allies to trying the Kaiser (who was forced to abdicate), but
the government of the Netherlands refused to hand him
over. He lived until 1941.

He kept us out of war

Presidential election slogan for Woodrow Wilson in 1916.
'He kept us out of war!' was said in a speech by Martin H.
Glynn, Governor of New York State, when praising Wilson
at the Democratic National Convention at St Louis (15 June
1916). Also **'Wilson's wisdom wins without war'**. These
slogans were true at the time they were coined (although
Wilson had nothing to do with them) but the following year
he did take the US into the First World War.

Help him finish the job

Conservative slogan beneath a photograph of Winston
Churchill on a poster at the General Election in 1945. The
argument did not prove persuasive. The phrase alluded to
words he had spoken in a radio broadcast (9 February 1941):
'Here is the answer which I will give to President Roosevelt
… Give us the tools, and we will finish the job.' Churchill's
prime objective at that time (Pearl Harbor did not take place
until December) was to bring the United States into the war
or, at least, to wring every possible ounce of assistance out of

it. Hence, the famous rallying cry with which he concluded. Another version was 'Send him back to finish the job.'

Here is the news and this is ―― reading it
During the Second World War, BBC radio newsreaders were allowed to identify themselves for the first time. This was so that, in case of invasion, listeners would be able to spot if the Germans had trained up their own team of fake BBC newsreaders. Well, that was the theory. This enabled the Yorkshire broadcaster Wilfred Pickles to personalize his bulletins by signing off with 'Good neet' and for Alvar Lidell to be parodied by *Beyond the Fringe* (in the 'The Aftermyth of War' sketch, 1961) as having introduced himself by saying, 'This is Alvar Lidell, bringing you news of fresh disasters.'

H-Hour
See under D-DAY.

H.I.L.T.H.Y.N.B.I.M.A. [How I love to hold your naked body in my arms]
Initialese used in correspondence between lovers in the Second World War.

Holocaust
Term applied to the mass murder of Jews and the attempted elimination of European Jewry by German Nazis during the Second World War. A holocaust is an all-consuming conflagration and is not perhaps the most obvious description of what happened to the estimated six million Jews under the Nazis, though many were burned after being

gassed or killed in some other way (compare FINAL
SOLUTION). The term seems to have arisen because 'genocide'
hardly sounds emotive enough. The popular use of 'the
Holocaust' for this purpose dates only from 1965, when
Alexander Donat published a book on the subject entitled
The Holocaust Kingdom. However, the *OED* has it in this
sense in the *News Chronicle* by 1942, as well as various other
1940s citations. As early as 1951, the Israeli Knesset had
'The Holocaust and Ghetto Uprising Day' – translated from
Yom ha-Sho'ah. The use was finally settled when a US TV
mini-series called *Holocaust* (1978) was shown and caused
controversy in many countries. Well before *that* happened,
Eric Partridge was advising in his *Usage and Abusage* (1947):
'Holocaust is "destruction by fire": do not synonymize it
with *disaster*. Moreover, it is properly an ecclesiastical
technicality.' In fact, the word derives from the Greek *holos*
and *kaustos* meaning 'wholly burnt' and was for many years
used to describe a sacrifice or offering that was burnt. Some
translations of the Bible use it to describe Abraham's
preparations to slay his son Isaac.

home front
Civilian participation in and contributions to the war effort,
in the Second World War, though the term had crept into
use towards the end of the First. 'Sir Archibald Sinclair
complained that the Government was concentrating its
energies too much on preparations for attack, to the neglect
of what was commonly known as "the home front" ' – *The
Annual Register 1937*. It was also known as **the domestic
front** by 1929.

Home Guard

The Local Defence Volunteers (LDV), formed in Britain at the outbreak of the Second World War, consisted of unpaid men of any age who mostly undertook modest guard and defence duties – though sometimes extending this to bomb disposal and manning ack-ack guns. They were soon renamed the Home Guard in the run-up to the threatened invasion. They may also have been nicknamed DAD'S ARMY.

how's your father

Used as a euphemism for sexual activity (as, 'indulging in a spot of how's your father'), this phrase seems to have been current in both world wars. It has been suggested that one source for the phrase might be George Robey's song 'In Other Words' (written by N. Ayer and C. Grey, 1916), which contains these lines: 'A student of nature, I walked down the Strand / And there a fair maiden did see. / I didn't know her, but she seemed to know me, / For she said, "How's your father?" to me.'

A comic song performed from the early 1940s by Flanagan and Allen in the character of a First World War veteran and his newly enlisted son contains the lines 'If a grey-haired lady asks "How's your father?", that'll be Madame Moselle' – obviously on the basis that she had been up to some 'how's your father' with the father long ago. This refers to the First World War song 'MADEMOISELLE FROM ARMENTIÈRES', which, however, does not appear to contain the actual expression 'How's your father?' in any of its several versions.

(Madam,) I am the civilization they are fighting to defend

Some man's famous response to a challenge as to why he was not at the Front during the First World War, fighting to defend civilization. Often ascribed – with how much justification, it is hard to say – to Heathcote William Garrod, a classical scholar and literary critic (1878–1960). It is so attributed by Dacre Balsdon in *Oxford Then and Now* (1970). Note how the line was incorporated in Hugh MacDiarmid's poem 'At the Cenotaph' (1935):

> 'Keep going to your wars, you fools, as of yore;
> I'm the civilisation you're fighting for.'

.

I shall return

During the Second World War, the American general Douglas MacArthur (1880–1964) was forced by the Japanese to pull out of the Philippines, leaving Corregidor on 11 March 1942. On 20 March he made his commitment to return when he arrived by train at Adelaide. He had journeyed southwards across Australia and was just about to set off eastwards for Melbourne. So, although he had talked in these terms before leaving the Philippines, his main statement was delivered not there but on Australian soil. At the station, a crowd awaited him, and prior to addressing them he had scrawled a few words on the back of an envelope: 'The President of the United States ordered me to break through the Japanese lines and proceed from Corregidor to Australia for the purpose, as I understand it, of organizing the American offensive against Japan, a primary object of which is the relief of the Philippines. I came through and I shall return.'

MacArthur had intended his first words to have the most impact – as a way of getting the war in the Pacific a higher priority – but it was his last three words that caught on. The Office of War Information tried to get him to amend them to '*We* shall return', foreseeing that there would be objections to a slogan which seemed to imply that he was all-important and that his men mattered little. MacArthur refused.

In fact, the phrase had first been suggested to a MacArthur aide in the form '*We* shall return' by a Filipino journalist, Carlos Romulo. 'America has let us down and won't be trusted,' Romulo had said. 'But the people still have confidence in MacArthur. If he says he is coming back, he will be believed.' The suggestion was passed to MacArthur, who adopted it – but adapted it.

MacArthur later commented: ' "I shall return" seemed a promise of magic to the Filipinos. It lit a flame that became a symbol which focused the nation's indomitable will and at whose shrine it finally attained victory and, once again, found freedom. It was scraped in the sands of the beaches, it was daubed on the walls of the *barrios*, it was stamped on the mail, it was whispered in the cloisters of the church. It became the battle cry of a great underground swell that no Japanese bayonet could still.'

As William Manchester wrote in *American Caesar* (1978): 'That it had this great an impact is doubtful … but unquestionably it appealed to an unsophisticated oriental people. Throughout the war American submarines provided Filipino guerillas with cartons of buttons, gum, playing cards, and matchboxes bearing the message.'

On 20 October 1944, MacArthur kept his promise and *did* return. Landing at Leyte, he said to a background of still-continuing gunfire: 'People of the Philippines, I have returned … By the grace of Almighty God, our forces stand again upon Philippine soil.'

I was only obeying orders

Much-parodied self-excusal from responsibility for one's actions, especially during and after the Second World War. The Charter of the International Military Tribunal at Nuremberg (1945–6) specifically excluded the traditional German defence of 'superior orders'. But the plea was, nevertheless, much advanced. As early as 1940, Rex Harrison said in the UK film *Night Train to Munich*: 'Captain Marsen was only obeying orders.' Kenneth Mars as a mad, Nazi-fixated playwright in *The Producers* (US 1967) said, 'I only followed orders!'

Not that everyone seemed aware of the parodying. From *The New York Times* (6 July 1983): 'Herbert Bechtold, a German-born officer in the [US] counter-intelligence [who became the "handler" of Klaus Barbie, the Nazi war criminal] was asked if he questioned the morality of hiring a man like Barbie by the United States. "I am not in a position to pass judgement on that," Mr Bechtold replied, "I was just following orders".'

I'm going down now, sir!

Of all the many catchphrases sired by the BBC radio show *ITMA*, the two with the most interesting origin were spoken by Horace Percival as 'the Diver'. They were derived from memories that the star of the show, Tommy Handley, had of an actual man who used to dive off the pier at New Brighton, on the River Mersey, in the 1920s/1930s. 'Don't forget the diver, sir, don't forget the diver,' the man would say, collecting money. 'Every penny makes the water warmer, sir.' The radio character first appeared in 1940 and no lift went down for the next few years without somebody using the Diver's main catchphrase or his other one, 'I'm going down now, sir! – which bomber pilots in the Second World War would also use when about to make a descent.

From *ITMA*'s VE Day edition (1945):

> *Effects: Knocking*
> *Handley:* 'Who's that knocking on the tank?'
> *The Diver:* 'Don't forget the diver, sir – don't forget the diver.'
> *Handley:* 'Lumme, it's Deepend Dan. Listen, as the war's over, what are you doing?'
> *The Diver:* 'I'm going down now, sir.'
> *Effects: Bubbles.*

Idle gossip sinks ships

See under WALLS HAVE EARS.

(Well) if you knows of a better 'ole – go to it

See OLD BILL.

In the name of God, go!

Words addressed to the flailing Prime Minister, Neville Chamberlain, in the House of Commons on 7 May 1940, by Leo S. Amery, the English Conservative politician (1873–1955).

At this date, criticism was growing of the British Government's handling of the war. Norway and Denmark had been lost to the Germans and yet a War Cabinet had not yet been formed. It was obvious that things were getting very bad indeed. In a dramatic speech, Amery said, 'Somehow or other we must get into the Government men who can match our enemies in fighting spirit' and he had considered quoting something that Oliver Cromwell had said to John Hampden 'some three hundred years ago, when this House found that its troops were being beaten again and again by the dash and daring of the Cavaliers', namely, 'We cannot go on being led as we are'. But, as Amery notes in his autobiography, he chose this other Cromwell remark instead.

'I was not out for a dramatic finish, but for a practical purpose; to bring down the Government if I could.' And so Amery quoted Cromwell's words when dismissing the Rump of the Long Parliament in 1653: 'You have sat too long here for any good you have been doing. Depart, I say, and let us have done with you. In the name of God, go!'

Chamberlain's government did indeed go. Churchill became Prime Minister and formed a National government three days later.

Intern the lot!

An informal British slogan in 1940, when 'the press was baying indiscriminately against all aliens' – Angus Calder, *The People's War* (1969).

iron rations

See EMERGENCY RATIONS.

Is Paris burning? [Brennt Paris?]

Following the D-Day landings on the northern coast of France in 1944, the next target was the liberation of Paris. The Allied forces managed to reach the French capital ahead of German Panzer divisions, which would have tried to destroy the city. When Hitler put this inquiry to Jodl at Oberkommando der Wehrmacht at Rastenberg (25 August 1944) – after Paris had been recaptured by the Allies – he received no reply. Later, the phrase was used as the title of a book by Collins and Lapierre (1965) and of a film (US 1965).

Is your journey really necessary?

Slogan first devised in 1939 to discourage evacuated civil servants from going home for Christmas. 'From 1941, the question was constantly addressed to all civilians, for, after considering a scheme for rationing on the "points" principle, or to ban all travel without a permit over more than fifty miles [80km], the government had finally decided to rely on voluntary appeals, and on making travel uncomfortable by reducing the number of trains' – Norman Longmate, *How We Lived Then* (1973). A poster drawn by Bert Thomas, on behalf of the 'Railway Executive Committee', showed a well-dressed couple with a little dog, thinking hard before approaching the window of a ticket office.

I.T.A.L.Y. [I treasure/trust and love you]

Lovers' acronym in correspondence, used to avoid military censorship and probably current by the time of the Second World War. Evelyn Waugh asked the Duchess of Devonshire (the youngest of the Mitford sisters) if she knew what it meant, in a 1956 letter.

I.T.M.A. [It's that man again]

Late 1930s catchphrase, often used in newspaper headlines and referring to Adolf Hitler, who was always bursting into the news with some territorial claim or other. Winston Churchill was to speak often of Hitler as 'that man'. It is appropriate that *ITMA*, the BBC radio programme incorporating more catchphrases per square minute than any other, before or since, should have had as its title an acronym based on a catchphrase. *ITMA* was first broadcast in July 1939 and ran until January 1949, when its star, Tommy Handley, died. What did the show consist of? There would be a knock on the famous *ITMA* door, a character would engage in a little banter with Tommy Handley, the catchphrase would be delivered (usually receiving a gigantic ovation), and then the next one would be wheeled in. Given this format, it is not easy now to appreciate why the show was so popular. But the laughter undoubtedly took people's minds off the war and the programmes brought together the whole country, fostering a family feeling and a sense of sharing which in turn encouraged the spread of catchphrases. The writing is not to everyone's taste nowadays (it relied heavily on weak rather than atrocious puns). However, Handley's brisk, cheerful personality was the magic ingredient that held the proceedings together. Characters came and went over the years, the cast fluctuated, and catchphrases changed. For specifically wartime catchphrases from the show, see I'M GOING DOWN NOW, SIR and THIS IS FUNF SPEAKING.

It might be you!
A Ministry of Health slogan on a poster of a woman with children in the Blitz, in the Second World War, coupled with the campaign's main slogan: 'Caring for evacuees is a national service'. Compare the much later slogan of the British National Lottery in the initial months after its launch in 1995: 'It Could Be YOU.' Ads featured a finger coming out of the sky and pointing at lucky winners.

It's a long way to Tipperary
A line from 'Tipperary', the most popular song among British soldiers during the early part of the First World War – though some say it was sung more in the music halls back home than at the Front. It was written just before the war, in 1912, and is credited to the British entertainer Jack Judge (1878–1938) and Harry Williams (1858–1930), though Judge later claimed to have written both words and music and given a credit to Williams in payment of a loan. The song tells of an Irishman on a visit to London who longs for the green fields of his home in southern Ireland. 'Goodbye Piccadilly! Farewell Leicester Square!' was soon

interpreted, however, as the British soldiers' farewell to the fleshpots of their homeland.

It's a long way to Tipperary
It's a long way to go;
It's a long way to Tipperary
To the sweetest girl I know!
Goodbye Piccadilly! Farewell, Leicester Square!
It's a long, long way to Tipperary,
But my heart's right there.

Japs

Slighting derogatory term for the Japanese in the Second
World War (sometimes 'dirty' was added). The word, as a
simple abbreviation for 'Japanese people', had been around
since at least the 1880s.

journey's end

This phrase became retrospectively linked to the First
World War when it was chosen by the English playwright
R.C. Sherriff (1896–1975) as the title of his 1929 play, set in
the trenches. It might seem to nod towards Shakespeare –
'Journeys end in lovers meeting' (*Twelfth Night*, II.iii.44) or
'Here is my journey's end' (*Othello*, V.ii.268) – or towards
Dryden, 'The world's an inn, and death the journey's end'
('Palamon and Arcite'). But it is impossible to be certain. In
his autobiography, *No Leading Lady* (1968), Sherriff wrote of
the titles he rejected, like 'Suspense' and 'Waiting', and then
added: 'One night I was reading a book in bed. I got to a
chapter that closed with the words: "It was late in the
evening when we came at last to our Journey's End". The
last two words sprang out as the ones I was looking for.
Next night I typed them on a front page for the play, and the
thing was done.' He does not say what the book was. It has
also been reported that Sherriff once explained that, in need
of a title, he saw an advertisement for a whiskey that
proclaimed, 'Have a dram at your journey's end …'

K.B.O. [keep buggering on]

This private motto ('We must just K.B.O.') was apparently used by Winston Churchill in 1940–41. It came to general attention when reported in Martin Gilbert, *Finest Hour* (1983), of which 'K.B.O.' is the title of the final chapter. Here it is taken from a use dating from December 1941, just after Pearl Harbor and when the United States had declared war on Germany and Italy, and vice versa. Churchill's use of the phrase was reported in a letter (dated 11 December) from one of his Private Secretaries, John Peck. However, it had already been reported in *The Diaries of Sir Robert Bruce Lockhart*, Vol. 2 (1973), where an exchange between Churchill and H.G. Wells at The Other Club is included in the entry for 24 June 1941:

> *Winston:* Ah, H.G., only one war aim for the present – K.B.O.
> *H.G.:* Please translate.
> *Winston:* Keep buggering on, of course.
> *H.G. (quick as lightning):* Ah, yes, Prime Minister, but you can't go on fighting rearguard actions all the time!

Kaiser Bill

Nickname of Kaiser Wilhelm II (1859–1941), German Emperor and King of Prussia (1888–1918). A jocular way of dealing with the enemy during the First World War. Cartoonists especially used the nickname, depicting the

K

Kaiser with an arrogant W-shaped moustache and a spiked helmet. A 'Kaiser' or 'Kaiser Bill' was a name for this type of moustache (by 1938).

kamikaze pilot

A kamikaze (from the Japanese *kami* – divine, godlike – and *kaze* – wind) was a Japanese suicide pilot who crashed his plane, carrying a bomb, and himself, into American ships and other targets during the Second World War. The word first became known in October 1944 when such pilots attacked American ships during the recapture of the Philippines. Apparently, 475 kamikaze planes hit Allied ships and 1,500 were shot down. Nine thousand were supposedly ready to resist the invasion fleet Japan was expecting at the war's end. According to the *OED*, the word was originally used in Japanese lore with reference to the supposed divine wind or 'wind of the gods' which blew on a night in August 1281, destroying the navy of the invading Mongols.

Keep calm and carry on

Photos of this poster slogan do not convey its powerful charm (except for the quietly authoritative crown on the top). When seen with the white capitals on a warm red background, the effect is not far short of sensational. According to an article in *The Guardian* (18 March 2009), the slogan's revival is down to a bookseller in Northumberland who came across an original copy of the poster in a box of old books he had purchased at auction. He and others have now sold tens of thousands of a

reproduction, the words seeming to strike a chord in
these troubled days. This is curious for two reasons.
Firstly, the poster was never actually released by the
Ministry of Information after it had been devised by an
anonymous official in the spring of 1939. The last in a
projected series of three, it was apparently held back for
when invasion was imminent. And, secondly, official
hectoring has never been well received by the British – as
witness the response to the two posters that did get
released, FREEDOM IS IN PERIL – DEFEND IT WITH ALL YOUR
MIGHT and YOUR COURAGE, YOUR CHEERFULNESS, YOUR
RESOLUTION WILL BRING US VICTORY.

The *Guardian* article carried this view of it from Dr
Lesley Prince, a social psychologist at the University of
Birmingham: 'It is a quiet, calm, authoritative, no-bullshit
voice of reason. It's not about British stiff upper lip, really.
This is saying, look, somebody out there knows what's
going on, and it'll be all right.'

Keep 'em flying!
Slogan in support of the US Air Force during the Second
World War, accompanying a poster by Harold N. Gilbert.
Another of his images coupled the slogan with 'Let's go!
U.S.A.', adding 'Uncle Sam Needs Pilots'.

(You know a vital secret?) Keep it dark
A security slogan in Britain during the Second World War.
The basic expression, meaning 'keep it secret', had been
around since 1681. As a wartime slogan, it appeared in more
than one formulation, and also in verse:

K

If you've news of our munitions
      KEEP IT DARK
Ships or planes or troop positions
      KEEP IT DARK
Lives are lost through conversation
Here's a tip for the duration
When you've private information
      KEEP IT DARK.

Shush, Keep It Dark was the title of a variety show running in London during September 1940, which suggests that the slogan must have been in use by that date. Later, the naval version of the BBC radio show *Merry Go Round* (1943–8) featured a character called Commander High-Price (Jon Pertwee) whose catchphrase was, 'Hush, keep it dark!'

Keep it under your hat
See WALLS HAVE EARS.

'Keep the Home Fires Burning'
Title of a song (1915) by the Welsh-born composer and actor Ivor Novello (1893–1951). It was originally entitled 'Till the Boys Come Home'. The lyrics were, in fact, written by Lena Guilbert Ford, though Novello is credited with the title line:

Keep the home fires burning
While your hearts are yearning,
Tho' your lads are far away
They dream of home.
There's a silver lining

Thro' the dark cloud shining,
Turn the dark cloud inside out,
Till the boys come home.

Kilroy was here

The most widely known of graffiti slogans. It was brought
to Europe by American GIs in about 1942 and was meant to
signify that 'a US serviceman was here' or 'a stranger was
here'. The phrase *may* have originated with James J. Kilroy
(died 1962), a shipyard inspector in Quincy, Massachusetts,
who would chalk it up to indicate that a check had been
made by him. It was also used as the title of a film (US 1947).

kitchen front

A more precise form of the HOME FRONT, emphasizing the
contribution to the war effort made by wives, mothers (and
others) who did their bit by providing food and domestic
comforts for those attempting to win the Second World
War. 'My sister writes of the many economical dishes she is
now able to prepare as a result of the B.B.C. talks on the
Kitchen Front' – *Punch* (3 September 1941).

'Knees Up, Mother Brown!'

Title of a song by R.P. Weston and Bert Lee (1939), which
was very popular in the Second World War and led to the
term 'a knees-up' for a lively celebration. *Collins English
Dictionary* (by the 1979 edition) defined the word as: 'A
boisterous dance involving the raising of alternate knees'.
Partridge/*Catch Phrases* gives the full phrase as a
catchphrase meaning 'Courage!' (which seems unlikely).

(winged) knights of the air

A name applied to the new breed of warriors – air-force pilots
on either opposing side – in the First World War and then in
the Second. In 1940–42, a short documentary film entitled
Knights of the Air was shown in cinemas to raise money for the
RAF Benevolent Fund. In a letter, the Battle of Britain RAF
pilot Richard Hillary wrote of his book *The Last Enemy*
(published in 1942): 'I got so sick of the stuff about our Island
Fortress and the Knights of the Air that I intended to write it
anyway … All this had been seen in the last war but that in
spite of that and not because of it, we still thought this one
worth fighting.' His objection to the phrase is somewhat
ironic in that he also saw pilot battles as a return to the days
of individual combat between two people, like knights of old.

knock-out blow

The final thrust that finishes the fight. As Secretary of State
for War, David Lloyd George gave an interview to Roy W.
Harris of the United Press of America. It was printed in *The
Times* (29 September 1915). Lloyd George was asked to 'give
the United Press, in the simplest possible language, the British
attitude toward the recent peace talk'. He answered: 'Sporting
terms are pretty well understood wherever English is spoken
… Well, then. The British soldier is a good sportsman …
Germany elected to make this a finish fight with England …
The fight must be to a finish – to a knock out.' In his memoirs,
Lloyd George entitled one chapter 'The Knock-out Blow' –
which is how the notion was popularly expressed. In boxing,
the expression had been known since the 1880s.

Lafayette, we are here! [Lafayette, nous voilà!]

Nine days after the American Expeditionary Force landed in France in 1917, Charles E. Stanton (1859–1933), a soldier and member of General Pershing's staff, stood at the tomb of Lafayette in the Picpus cemetery in Paris, and declared, 'Here and now, in the presence of the illustrious dead, we pledge our hearts and our honour in carrying this war to a successful issue. Lafayette, we are here!' This graceful tribute to the Marquis de Lafayette (1757–1834), who enlisted with the American revolutionary armies in 1777 and forged a strong emotional link between the United States and France, was delivered by Colonel Stanton on 4 July 1917 and repeated on 14 July. According to *The New York Tribune* (6 September 1917), Stanton may have spoken all or some of his remarks in French – *Lafayette, nous voilà!* As *Bartlett's Familiar Quotations* (1968 and 1980 editions) points out, the remark has also been attributed to General Pershing himself, though he disclaimed having said 'anything so splendid'. There is a suggestion, however, that he may have pronounced the phrase before Stanton and that Stanton merely picked it up.

(The) lamps are going out all over Europe

Sir Edward Grey (later Viscount Grey of Fallodon) (1862–1933) was Foreign Secretary at the outbreak of the First World War and with this statement tolled the knell for the era that was about to pass. In *Twenty-five Years* (1925), he recounted: 'A friend came to see me on one of the

L

evenings of the last week – he thinks it was on Monday
August 3. We were standing at a window of my room in the
Foreign Office. It was getting dusk, and the lamps were
being lit in the space below on which we were looking. My
friend recalls that I remarked on this with the words, "The
lamps are going out all over Europe; we shall not see them
lit again in our lifetime".'

(A) land fit for heroes (sometimes country fit for heroes)
A semi-official political slogan after the First World War.
When it was over, Prime Minister David Lloyd George
gave rise to this slogan in a speech at Wolverhampton on
24 November 1918, the exact words of which were: 'What is
our task? To make Britain a fit country for heroes to live in.'
By 1921, with wages falling in all industries, the sentiment
was frequently recalled and mocked.

Lebensraum [living room/space]
Territory which the Germans believed they needed to
acquire for their natural development – a major component
of Nazi ideology and its expansionist policies. A name
applied from the early 1900s.
    '*Lebensraum*, or a place in the sun, is the historic claim
and ambition of Germany, as "encirclement" is her historic
anxiety' – Arthur Salter, *The Dual Policy* (1939).

Lest we forget
Rudyard Kipling's poem 'Recessional' (1897) was written as
a warning on Queen Victoria's Jubilee Day that while
empires pass away, God lives on. It ends:

The tumult and the shouting dies;
The captains and the kings depart:
Still stands Thine ancient sacrifice,
An humble and a contrite heart.
Lord God of hosts, be with us yet,
Lest we forget – lest we forget!

Kipling himself may have agreed to the adoption of 'Lest we forget' as an epitaph during his work for the Imperial War Graves Commission after the First World War.

Let's get on wiv it!

Catchphrase of the British husband-and-wife entertainers, Nat Mills (1900–93) and Bobbie (d. 1955). They flourished in the 1930s and 1940s portraying 'a gumpish type of lad and his equally gumpish girlfriend'. Nat recalled in a letter to me (in 1979): 'It was during the very early part of the war. We were booked by the BBC to go to South Wales for a *Workers' Playtime*. Long tables had been set up in front of the stage for the workers to have lunch on before the broadcast. On this occasion, a works foreman went round all the tables shouting, "Come on, let's get on with it," to get them to finish their lunch on time. I was informed he used this phrase so many times, the workers would mimic him among themselves. So I said to Bobbie, "You start the broadcast by talking to yourself and I'll interject and say, 'Let's get on with it'." Lo and behold it got such a yell of laughter we kept it in all our broadcasts. Even Churchill used our slogan to the troops during the early part of the war.' According to Nat's obituary in *The Times* (14 August

L

1993), the phrase was 'whinnied in a weird whine and imitated by everyone who ever heard them on the wireless in the war years.'

Let us go forward together
A Government morale-building slogan in use by 1940. A direct quotation from Churchill's first speech on becoming Prime Minister (13 May 1940): 'I say, "Come then, let us go forward together with our united strength".' On a poster, it was used to accompany his picture, in bulldog pose but wearing a trilby hat, with tanks and Spitfires behind him. Churchill's collected speeches show that he subsequently repeated the phrase some dozen times, for example: 'Let us go forward together in all parts of the Empire, in all parts of the Island' (speaking on the war, 27 January 1940). But it was not new to him even then: 'I can only say to you let us go forward together and put these grave matters to the proof' (conclusion of a speech on Ulster, 14 March 1914).

(the) Liberation
The driving out of the Germans from France by the Allies in 1944 (*La Libération*). 'Liberation' rather than 'capture' or 'invasion' or 'occupation' was the key word that President Roosevelt insisted should be used, at a press conference in May 1944, one month before the D-Day landings.

Liberty ——
Amid the heightened anti-German feeling of the First World War, many German names or words were changed or adapted. In the US, patriotic fervour led to sauerkraut being

renamed 'Liberty cabbage' (recalled in 1927) and German measles, 'Liberty measles'. (An echo of this was to be heard in 2003 during the US invasion of Iraq, when dismay at French opposition to the move led to US patriots supposedly renaming french fries as 'Liberty fries'.)

lions for lambs

The title of the film *Lions for Lambs* (US 2007) was intended to suggest that Allied forces in the then current unpleasantness in Iraq were directed by a flock of sheep in the Pentagon and the White House. At first, it seemed as if this use was making rather a mess of the remark that British troops were, rather, 'LIONS LED BY DONKEYS' during the First World War (see next entry). However, this now seems not to be the case. In the film, a college professor played by Robert Redford condemns the apathy of the American public towards world events and, specifically, the War on Terror. He encourages one promising but disaffected student to feel a sense of personal responsibility and take action against politicians and military leaders who are all too willing to see the deaths of soldiers as a negligible cost of the war. To illustrate his point, the professor tells the student that during the First World War, hundreds of thousands of British soldiers died in futile attacks on deeply entrenched German troops. The German soldiers came to admire their counterparts so much that they wrote poems and stories praising their bravery. They also derided the arrogant incompetence of the British Army officers who, safely in the rear, held high teas as young men were needlessly sacrificed. One such observation was 'Nowhere have I seen such lions

L

led by such lambs' [*Ich habe noch nie solchen Lowen gesehen die solche Lamer gefuhrt werden*]. This may have been made by an anonymous infantryman during the Battle of the Somme or by General Max von Gallwitz, Supreme Commander of the German forces. In either case, it may be derived from Alexander the Great's proclamation, 'I am never afraid of an army of Lions led into battle by a Lamb. I fear more the army of Lambs who have a Lion to lead them.'

The above is based on an anonymous article in the online edition of *The Times* (16 October 2007).

lions led by donkeys

This description of British led and leaders seems likely to have made its earliest appearance in the form 'lions commanded by asses', something said by a Russian soldier during the Crimean War (1853–6). Then in an 1871 book about the Siege of Paris, the phrase came out as 'lions led by asses' (or 'jackasses'), apparently a reference to a description in *The Times* (London). But the most significant use was claimed to have been during the First World War and provided Alan Clark with a title, *The Donkeys*, for his book (1961) about British generals in that conflagration. As his epigraph, Clark quoted a supposed exchange between the German generals Erich Ludendorff and Max Hoffman. The latter succeeded Ludendorff as chief of the German general staff in 1916:

> *Ludendorff:* The English soldiers fight like lions.
> *Hoffman:* True. But don't we know that they are lions led by donkeys?

Clark gives the source as Field Marshal von Falkenhayn's memoirs – but the exchange remains untraced to this day, not least in Falkenhayn's memoirs. Indeed, it is now abundantly clear that Clark made the source up and, in his lifetime, headed off all attempts to locate the provenance of the phrase that gave him the punchy title for his book.

listening post (sometimes forward listening post)
'A concealed or underground position in No–Man's Land where two or more men would keep vigil through the night with two or three reliefs' in order to detect the disposition and any movements of the enemy – Partridge/*Long Trail.* By 1916.

Loose talk costs lives
See WALLS HAVE EARS.

Lord Haw-Haw
See GERMANY CALLING, GERMANY CALLING!

lost generation
The American poet Gertrude Stein recorded and popularized a remark made by a French garage owner in the Midi just after the First World War. Rebuking an apprentice who had made a shoddy repair to Stein's car, he said: 'All you young people who served in the war' are from 'a lost generation' [*une génération perdue*]. Ernest Hemingway used the remark as the epigraph to his novel *The Sun Also Rises* (1926) and referred to it again in *A Moveable Feast* (1964). I would guess, however, that the phrase is now more often

L

used to refer to the large number of promising young men who lost their lives in the First World War rather than, as in Stein's context, to those who were not killed in the war but who survived to become part of a generation that was thought to have lost its values.

John Keegan's *The First World War* (1998) begins by analysing the casualties and says of the small percentages of national populations killed or wounded: 'Even those smaller proportions left terrible psychic wounds, falling as they did on the youngest and most active sections of society's males. It has, as the war recedes into history, become fashionable to decry the lament for this "Lost Generation" as myth-making.' Here Keegan equates the 'Lost Generation' with those men killed or wounded, rather than all those men who wasted their youth in the war, which is what Gertrude Stein meant. A further redefinition of the phrase occurs in an F. Scott Fitzgerald short story, 'The Swimmers', published in *The Saturday Evening Post* (19 October 1929): 'There was a lost generation in the saddle at the moment, but it seemed to him that the men coming on, the men of the war, were better.' So that makes the lost generation the men of *before* the First World War.

Luftwaffe
Name for the German air force before and during the Second World War (literally the word means 'air weapon'). (The name of the airline Lufthansa, formed after the First World War, means something like 'air association'.)

'Mademoiselle from Armentières' [sometimes Anglicized as Armenteers]

The title of a bawdy song that was sung during the First World War. It begins, mildly:

> Mademoiselle from Armentières, *Parlez-vous*
> Mademoiselle from Armentières, *Parlez-vous*,
> Mademoiselle from Armentières,
> She hasn't been kissed for forty years,
> *Chorus:* Hinky-dinky, *parlez-vous!* [or Inky-pinky *parley-vous!*].

As to who might have written the lyrics for this song, this is in dispute. It might have been Edward Rowland and a Canadian composer, Lt. Glitz Rice, or it might have been Harry Carlton and Joe Tunbridge. A third claimant is the British songwriter 'Harry Wincott' (Alfred Walden). Red Rowley is also credited with updating what was an old song even at the start of the First World War. The tune of the song was believed to have been popular in the French Army in the 1830s. The original words told of an encounter between an innkeeper's daughter named Mademoiselle de Bar le Luc, and two German officers. The tune was resurrected during the Franco-Prussian war of 1870 and again early in the First World War. *Mademoiselle from Armentières* was also the name of a 1926 movie. Armentières became very familiar to British and other forces as a centre of R. and R. Other songs to the same tune include 'The

Sergeant-Major's Having a Time' and 'A German Officer Crossed the Rhine'. During the Second World War, the comic duo Flanagan and Allen had a hit with 'Mademoiselle from Armentières' in 1940, but with different music and lyrics written by Ted Waite (see HOW'S YOUR FATHER) and referring to the original song.

Mae West
An inflatable life-jacket, issued to the Services in the Second World War and known as such by 1939. The nickname was coined by the RAF in tribute to the curvaceous American film star (1892–1980) and then adopted as the official description, with the full approval of the busty lady. Said she, 'I've been in *Who's Who* and I know what's what but this is the first time I've ever been in a dictionary' – quoted in her book *Goodness Had Nothing To Do With It*, Chap. 17 (1959). 'A life-saving waistcoat … can be inflated in a few moments by the wearer, and for some obscure reason is known technically as a "Mae West" ' – *The Listener* (11 January 1940).

Make do and mend
Phrase popularized during the Second World War, when there were Make-Do-and-Mend sections in some department stores. It was designed to encourage thrift and the repairing of old garments, furniture, etc., rather than expenditure of scarce resources on making new. It was possibly derived from 'make and mend', which was a Royal Navy term for an afternoon free from work and devoted to mending clothes. On one official poster, it is spelt 'Make-do and Mend'.

master race

Hitler first started calling his 'Aryan race' the 'super race' in his book *Mein Kampf* (1924). He dictated the book to Rudolf Hess while they were both in prison for plotting to take over Bavaria. It was, however, Hitler's propaganda chief, Josef Goebbels, who started promoting this supposed Aryan race as 'the master race' from about 1929. The term had been in use since the mid-19th century.

merchants of death

Merchants of Death was the title of a 1920 book by H.C. Engelbrecht and F.D. Hanighan. It advanced the view that munitions-makers and others who profited from US involvement in the First World War had been prime causes of it.

mightier yet

Words extracted from A.C. Benson's lyric for Edward Elgar's patriotic anthem 'Land of Hope and Glory' (which had become popular by the time of the First World War). The phrase was used on a morale-building Second World War poster showing battleships, but was withdrawn when it was discovered that people failed to get the literary allusion:

> Land of Hope and Glory, Mother of the Free,
> How shall we extol thee, who are born of thee?
> Wider still and wider shall thy bounds be set;
> God who made thee mighty, make thee mightier yet.

moaning Minnie

In the First World War, a 'Minnie' was the slang name for a German *Minenwerfer* (literally, 'mine thrower'), a trench mortar or the shell that came from it, making a distinctive moaning noise. In the Second World War, the name was applied to air-raid sirens that also made a moaning sound.

Molotov cocktail

This incendiary device, similar to a petrol bomb, acquired its name in Finland during the early days of the Second World War and was known as such by 1940. V.M. Molotov had become Soviet Minister for Foreign Affairs in 1939. The Russians invaded Finland and these home-made grenades proved an effective way for the Finns to oppose their tanks. 'When the soldiers attack the Russian tanks, they call their rudely made hand grenades "Molotov's cocktails"' – Walter Citrine, *My Finnish Diary* (1940).

(a) more efficient conduct of the war

A phrase from the First World War, though it had been used in several previous ones – usually when someone new was taking charge and promising to make a better job of it. A.J.P. Taylor, in his *English History 1914–45* (1965), has: 'The Coalition government, which Asquith announced on 26 May 1915, claimed to demonstrate national unity and to promote a more efficient conduct of the war.' Writing of the following year – 1916 – in *Clementine Churchill* (1979), Mary Soames has 'more vigorous and efficient prosecution of the war'. Is it also sometimes given as 'more energetic' conduct? Compare, from Lord Home, *The Way the Wind Blows* (1976):

'Sir Roger Keyes [in 1939] … made an impassioned speech in favour of more urgent conduct of the war.'

Morrison shelter
Known initially – by February 1941 – as a 'Morrison table shelter', this was an indoor air-raid shelter made of steel and shaped like a table. It was named after Herbert Morrison (1888–1965) when he was Home Secretary and Minister of Home Security (1940–45). 'Yesterday Mrs Churchill, Mr Morrison and Miss Ellen Wilkinson tested the comfort of the first Morrison Table Shelter' – *Daily Herald* (12 February 1941). Compare ANDERSON (SHELTER).

muddling through
Supposedly what the British have a great talent for. *H.L. Mencken's Dictionary of Quotations* (1942) has this citation: 'The English always manage to muddle through' – 'author unidentified; first heard *circa* 1885'. Ira Gershwin celebrated the trait in the song 'Stiff Upper Lip' from *A Damsel in Distress* (1937). He remembered the phrase 'keep muddling through' from much use at the time of the First World War, but knew that it had first been noted in a speech by John Bright MP *circa* 1864 (though, ironically, Bright was talking about the Northern States in the American Civil War). The *OED* defines 'to muddle through' as: 'to attain one's object by good fortune rather than good management.'

Nach Paris! [To Paris!]

A German slogan at the start of the First World War. The move was not accomplished until the Second World War.

(Their) name liveth for evermore

The standard epitaph put over lists of the dead after the First World War. It was chosen by Rudyard Kipling, who had been invited by the Imperial War Graves Commission to devise memorial texts for the dead. He admitted to 'naked cribs of the Greek anthology' and also used biblical texts, as here. Ecclesiasticus 44:14 reads: 'Their bodies are buried in peace; but their name liveth for evermore.'

Napoo/Nah poo

See GOOD-BYE-EE!

(The) Navy's here!

Phrase indicating that rescue is at hand; everything is going to be all right; be assured. From an actual use of the words during the Second World War. On the night of 16 February 1940, 299 British seamen were freed from captivity aboard the German ship *Altmark* as it lay in a Norwegian fjord. The destroyer *Cossack*, under the command of Captain Philip Vian, had managed to locate the German supply ship and a boarding party discovered that British prisoners were locked in its hold. As Vian described it, Lieutenant Bradwell Turner, leader of the boarding party, called out: 'Any British down there?' 'Yes, we're all British,' came the reply. 'Come

N

on up then,' he said, 'The Navy's here.' The identity of the speaker is still in some doubt, however. *The Times* on 19 February 1940 gave a version from the lips of one of those who had been freed and who had actually heard the exchange: 'John Quigley of London said that the first they knew of their rescue was when they heard a shout of "Any Englishmen here?" They shouted "Yes" and immediately came the cheering words, "Well, the Navy is here." Quigley said – "We were all hoarse with cheering when we heard those words".'

Nazi

A member of the National Socialist German Workers' Party, *Nationalsozialistisch Deutsche Arbeiterpartei*, of which this is a shortening. The party was developed from 1920 under the leadership of Adolf Hitler and Ernst Roehm. The abbreviation was in use by 1930 and often loosely applied to any member of the German Government or military in the period 1933–45. Initially, it was used by opponents of the party. Later, it became the 'hate' word in Britain and, in his many speeches during the Second World War, Winston Churchill pronounced it with particular venom (as though it were somehow related to 'nasty').

Nazi jackboot

Phrase used to encapsulate the horrors of Nazism and the British attitude towards it in the Second World War. 'Either the British way shall survive or the Nazi jackboot and whip shall take its place' – *R.A.F. Journal* (2 May 1942); 'Looking back on that visit of the late forties, I had not appreciated just how recently those Nazi jackboots had strutted down the Champs-Elysées' – *The Herald* (Glasgow) (23 August 1994); 'We may learn from Janus and Janus that 11 per cent of American men and women have had personal experience of dominance/bondage, but instead of that news satisfying our curiosity, it merely prompts more detailed questions … Are Nazi jackboots still in favour?' – *The Independent on Sunday* (25 April 1993).

Never again

General-purpose anti-war slogan but used specifically with regard to Germany in the First World War from 1915. T.F.A. Smith wrote in *The Soul of Germany* (1915): 'The oft-quoted phrase is applicable to the case: Never again!' David Lloyd George said in a newspaper interview: ' "Never again" has become our battle cry' – *The Times* (29 September 1916). Winston Churchill, in *The Second World War* (Vol. 1, 1948), says of the French: 'With one passionate spasm [they cried] never again.' Compare the German *'Nie wieder Krieg* [Never again war]', a slogan of the 1920s–1930s.

Never give in

There is a slight question mark over how much currency this expression had during the Second World War but it certainly had some – and thereafter. President George W. Bush's speechwriters sometimes gave him recycled Churchillisms to spout: 'Against such an enemy, there's only one effective response: We never back down, never give in and never accept anything less than complete victory' – speech to the National Endowment for Democracy in

N

Washington DC (6 October 2005). So what was the
Churchill original? On 29 October 1941, the Prime Minister
cheered himself up by returning to his old school, Harrow,
for the traditional songs. In his speech to the boys, he said:
'Never give in. Never give in. Never, never, never, never – in
nothing, great or small, large or petty – never give in,
except to convictions of honour and good sense. Never yield
to force. Never yield to the apparently overwhelming might
of the enemy.'

night and fog [Nacht und Nebel]
This chilling euphemistic phrase was the name of a 1941
decree issued over Hitler's signature describing a simple
process: that anyone suspected of a crime against occupying
German forces was to disappear into 'night and fog'. Such
people were thrown into the concentration camp system, in
most cases never to be heard of again. Alain Resnais, the
French film director, made a cinema short about a
concentration camp and called it *Nuit et Brouillard* (1955).
Although there might seem to be an echo in the title of
Woody Allen's film *Shadows and Fog* (1992), that alludes
rather to features of German expressionist films of the
1920s and 1930s.

The phrase comes from Wagner's opera *Das Rheingold*
(1869). '*Nacht und Nebel niemand gleich*' is the spell that
Alberich puts on the magic Tarnhelm, which renders him
invisible and omnipresent. It means approximately, 'In night
and fog no one is seen' or 'night and fog is the same as being
no one, a non-person' or 'night and fog make you no one
instantly'.

(The) night is your friend, the 'V' is your sign

During the Second World War the Resistance movements in occupied Europe were encouraged from London by broadcasts over the BBC. 'Colonel Britton' was the *nom de guerre* of Douglas Ritchie (1905–67), a British propagandist. In an English-language broadcast on 31 July 1941, he began: 'It's about the "V" – the sign of victory – that I want to talk to you now. All over Europe the V-sign is seen by the Germans and to the Germans and the Quislings it is indeed the writing on the wall. It is the sign which tells them that one of the unknown soldiers has passed that way. And it's beginning to play on their nerves. They see it chalked on pavements, pencilled on posters, scratched on the mudguards of German cars. Flowers come up in the shape of a "V"; men salute each other with the V-sign separating their fingers. The number five is a "V" and men working in the fields turn to the village clocks as the chimes sound the hour of five.'

In the same broadcast, the 'Colonel' also encouraged the use of the 'V' in Morse Code, three short taps and a heavy one: 'When you knock on a door, there's your knock. If you call a waiter in a restaurant, call him like this: "Eh, *garçon!*" [*taps rhythm on wine glass*] ... Tell all your friends about it and teach them the "V" sound. If you and your friends are in a café and a German comes in, tap out the V-sign all together.' The Morse Code for 'V' is also the rhythm of the opening phrase of Beethoven's Symphony No. 5, and the musical phrase was used in BBC broadcasts to occupied Europe to reinforce the message.

From these broadcasts emerged an evocative slogan: 'You wear no uniforms and your weapons differ from ours –

N

but they are not less deadly. The fact that you wear no uniforms is your strength. The Nazi official and the German soldier don't know you. But they fear you … The night is your friend. The "V" is your sign.' (Cole Porter's song 'All Through the Night', 1934, had earlier contained the lines: 'The day is my enemy / The night is my friend.') Hence, presumably, later, *The Night Was Our Friend*, title of a play (1950) by Michael Pertwee.

These kinds of broadcasts were also used for sending coded messages to Resistance workers in France: '*Le lapin a bu un apéritif*', '*Mademoiselle caresse le nez de son chien*', and '*Jacqueline sait le latin*' are examples of signals used to trigger sabotage operations or to warn of parachute drops.

night of broken glass [Kristallnacht]
Euphemism attributed to Walther Funk to describe the Nazi pogrom against Jews in Germany on the night of 9–10 November 1938.

night of the long knives
Phrase for any kind of surprise purge (but one in which, usually, no actual blood is spilt). It was applied, for example, to Harold Macmillan's wholesale reorganization of his Cabinet in 1962. When Norman St John Stevas was dropped from his Cabinet post in a 1981 reshuffle, one wit described the changes as Mrs Thatcher's 'night of the long hatpin'. The original was *die Nacht der langen Messer* in Nazi Germany. During the weekend of 29 June–2 July 1934, Hitler, aided by Himmler's black-shirted SS, liquidated the leadership of the brown-shirted SA. These latter

undisciplined storm troopers had helped Hitler gain power but were now getting in the way of his dealings with the German Army. Some 83 were murdered on the pretext that they were plotting another revolution. 'It was no secret that this time the revolution would have to be bloody,' Hitler explained to the Reichstag on 13 July. 'When we spoke of it, we called it "The Night of the Long Knives" … in every time and place, rebels have been killed … I ordered the leaders of the guilty shot. I also ordered the abscesses caused by our internal and external poisons cauterised until the living flesh was burned.' It seems that in using the phrase, Hitler may have been quoting from an early Nazi marching song.

Compare, *Verschwörung der langen Messer* ('conspiracy of the long knives', translating the much older Welsh phrase *twyll y cyllvyll hirion*) that had previously been used as the name of a premeditated massacre of unarmed and unprepared men. To be precise it described the supposed murder by Hengist and his Saxons of a party of British nobles at a peace conference, using knives hidden in their shoes, as described by Nennius, Geoffrey of Monmouth, and various other pseudo-historical sources. The German phrase is used in Geoffrey of Monmouth's *Historia Regum Britanniae*, ed. San-Marte (1854).

(There are) no atheists in (the) foxholes

A saying from the Second World War, implying that when the heat is on, any soldier is ready to believe in some higher power. Various people are credited with the coinage but the most likely is an American priest, William Thomas

Cummings (1903–45). He is reported to have said it in a
field sermon at Bataan in 1942 and is so quoted by Carlos
P. Romulo in *I Saw the Fall of the Philippines* (1943), although
the phrase is used in the film *Wake Island*, which was
released in that same year.

The term 'foxhole' to describe a slit trench or any hole in
the ground in which a soldier takes refuge was current by
1919 and is probably of American origin.

Atheist organizations have predictably come out against
the aphorism. James Morrow commented: ' "There are no
atheists in foxholes" isn't an argument against atheism, it's
an argument against foxholes.'

No guts, no glory

It has been reported that when playing golf, people will
sometimes say to themselves, before trying a difficult shot:
'No guts, no glory', occasionally followed by, 'No failure, no
story.' *The New York Times* of 30 August 1945 has it; the
Scribner Dictionary of Soldier Talk (1984) has it as Second
World War slang; and Partridge/*Slang* has simply 'No guts!'
– 'a derisive exhortation' since the 1920s. 'No gut, no glory!'
was used as a promotional tag for the film *The Incredibles*
(US 2004), referring presumably to the overweight
superman hero.

no man's land

A phrase for unowned, waste land (current by 1320), but
more recently used to describe the space between
entrenched armies, as in the First World War. Partridge/
Long Trail comments: 'A strangely romantic name for the

area between the front line trenches of either army, held by neither but patrolled, at night, by both.'

No more bloody wars, no more bloody medals!

During the First World War, Queen Mary is said to have been presenting medals to a regiment back from the Front. She had just pinned a medal on one soldier's chest and as she was passing on down the line, she overheard him say, rather ungratefully, to the person standing next to him, 'No more bloody wars for me, mate!' Whereupon, quick as a flash, Queen Mary turned to the soldier with a withering glance and said, 'That's fine by me, my man. No more bloody wars, no more bloody medals!' This story was told by Robert Lacey on BBC Radio's *Quote … Unquote* (19 February 1979). In 2010, he added: 'The "No more bloody wars, No more bloody medals" story comes from my father, Leonard John "Bill" Lacey, a loyal member of the Ewhurst, Surrey, Home Guard in the 1940s. I do not think that he personally heard Queen Mary make the remark, but he repeated it often enough to turn it into history so far as I am concerned.'

No more war

An age-old cry. 'No, no, no more war! Let us not sink ourselves so many more millions in debt' – James Boswell reporting a coffee-house conversation (diary entry for 11 December 1762). But A.J.P. Taylor, in his *English History 1914—45*, suggests that the slogan was 'irresistible' at the end of the First World War. A.G. McDonell, *England, Their England*, Chap. 1 (1933) talks of No More War as 'the name of an ardent society of left-wing pacifists'. Indeed, a group of such (including Bertrand Russell and Bernard Shaw) were signatories of a letter to the *Manchester Guardian* (9 March 1922) urging ' "No More War" Demonstrations' on the anniversary of the 'outbreak of war' – 'the sole object will be to express the general longing for peace.' The phrase was used by Winston Churchill at the end of a letter to Lord Beaverbrook in 1928 (quoted in Martin Gilbert's biography of Churchill, Vol. 5). In *Goodbye to Berlin* (1939), Christopher Isherwood describes a Nazi book-burning. The books are from a 'small liberal pacifist publisher'. One of the Nazis holds up a book called *Nie wieder Krieg* [Never again war] as though it were 'a nasty kind of reptile'. 'No More War!' a fat, well-dressed woman laughs scornfully and savagely, 'What an idea!'

(the) noise and the people!
A famous phrase describing what it was like to be in battle, but in which world war? According to the *Oxford Dictionary of Quotations* (1979), quoting the *Hudson Review* (Winter, 1951), a certain Captain Strahan exclaimed, 'Oh, my dear fellow, the noise ... and the people!' after the Battle of Bastogne in 1944. Various correspondents have suggested it was earlier in that war, however. Roy T. Kendall wrote (1986): 'I heard this phrase used, in a humorous manner, during the early part of 1942. It was related to me as having been said by a young Guards officer, newly returned from Dunkirk [1940], who on being asked what it was like used the expression – the inference being, a blasé attitude to the dangers and a disdain of the common soldiery he was forced to mix with.' Tony Bagnall Smith added that the Guards

officer was still properly dressed and equipped when he said it, and that his reply was, rather: 'My dear, the noise and the people – how they smelt!'

The *ODQ* (1992) appears to have come round to the earlier use regarding Dunkirk, in the form 'The noise, my dear! And the people!' and finds it already being quoted in Anthony Rhodes, *Sword of Bone*, Chap. 22 (1942).

Another originator is said to be Lord Sefton, a Guards officer at Dunkirk (suggested in correspondence in *The London Review of Books* beginning on the 29 October 1998). In the same correspondence, an assertion reappeared that it was something said by the actor Ernest Thesiger at a dinner party in 1919 regarding his experiences as a soldier in the battle of the Somme.

N.O.R.W.I.C.H. [(K)nickers off ready when I come home]
Lovers' acronym for use in correspondence and to avoid military censorship. Possibly in use by the time of the First World War, according to Eric Partridge.

not forgotten
In 1919, a year after the Armistice which ended the First World War, Miss Marta Cunningham, a singer, was visiting her local hospital. She asked the matron if, by chance, she still had any wounded servicemen under treatment. 'Six hundred' came the bleak reply. The singer was horrified and soon discovered that in fact there were many thousands of badly wounded men lying in hospitals up and down the country, bored, lonely, and in pain. Miss Cunningham

N

established the Not Forgotten Association in 1920 with the object of providing entertainment and recreation for the hopelessly war crippled – anything to alleviate the tedium of their lives and give them something to which they could look forward. In 1926 the Association officially defined its task as being 'to provide comfort, cheer and entertainment for the wounded ex-servicemen still in hospital as a result of the Great War'. As the years went on the Association, which still exists and provided the foregoing information, has adapted to meet changing needs and extended its activities to include those wounded in more recent conflicts.

Nuts!

In December 1944, the Germans launched a counter-offensive in what came to be known as the BATTLE OF THE BULGE. Anthony C. McAuliffe, the American general (1898–1975) (nicknamed OLD CROCK), was acting commander of the American 101st Airborne Division and was ordered to defend the strategic town of Bastogne in the Ardennes forest. This was important because Bastogne stood at a Belgian crossroads through which the advancing armies had to pass. When the Americans had been surrounded like 'the hole in a doughnut' for seven days, the Germans said they would accept a surrender. On 23 December, McAuliffe replied: 'Nuts!'

The Germans first of all interpreted this one-word reply as meaning 'crazy' and took time to appreciate what they were being told. Encouraged by McAuliffe's spirit, his men managed to hold the line and thus defeat the last major enemy offensive of the war.

McAuliffe recounted the episode in a BBC broadcast on 3 January 1945: 'When we got [the surrender demand] we thought it was the funniest thing we ever heard. I just laughed and said, "Nuts", but the German major who brought it wanted a formal answer; so I decided – well, I'd just say "Nuts", so I had it written out: "QUOTE, TO THE GERMAN COMMANDER: NUTS. SIGNED, THE AMERICAN COMMANDER UNQUOTE".'

When Agence France Presse sought a way of translating this, it resorted to *'Vous n'êtes que de vieilles noix'* [You are only old fogeys] – although *'noix'* in French slang also carries the same testicular meaning as 'nuts' in English. When McAuliffe's obituary came to be written, *The New York Times* observed: 'Unofficial versions strongly suggest that the actual language used by the feisty American general was considerably stronger and more profane than the comparatively mild "Nuts", but the official version will have to stand.'

O valiant hearts

Phrase from 'The Supreme Sacrifice' (1919), a hymn with words by the English lawyer and poet Sir John S. Arkwright (1872–1954). In the 1930s this moving hymn suffered a backlash and was dropped from Remembrance Day services by those who believed it was insufficiently critical of militarism. The hymn contains *OED*'s earliest citation for the phrase 'supreme sacrifice' which, alas, became a cliché for death in war:

> O valiant hearts, who to your glory came
> Through dust of conflict and through battle flame;
> Tranquil you lie, your knightly virtue proved,
> Your memory hallowed in the land you loved.
>
> Proudly you gathered, rank on rank, to war,
> As who had heard God's message from afar;
> All you had hoped for, all you had, you gave
> To save mankind – yourselves you scorned to save.

occupation

First used (in English and in French) to describe the occupation of northern France by the Germans in 1940. Later used to describe the occupation of any country by them. Not to be confused with such uses as 'Army of Occupation' – the name given to the American force in the Mexican-American War and in Germany after the First World War.

offensive

By the second half of the 19th century, this term was already in use to describe a large-scale military attack with a specific objective. However, it has a marked First World War air to it. 'A strong offensive in the West might induce the Allies to make a premature counter-attack' – John Buchan, *Nelson's History of the War*, Chap. 13 (1916). Partridge/*Long Trail* adds: 'Also used by GHQ in 1916–17 for a frame of mind it desired to encourage in front-line troops in order to weaken the enemy's confidence.'

Oh! It's a lovely war!

'Oh! It's a Lovely War!' was the title of a brisk, jolly song – albeit laced with irony – that was popular with soldiers in the First World War. The second exclamation mark was not, however, included on the cover of the sheet music. The song was written by J.P. Long and M. Scott and the chorus goes:

> Oh, oh, oh, it's a lovely war,
> Who wouldn't be a soldier, eh? Oh, it's a shame to take the pay.
> As soon as reveille has gone we feel just as heavy as lead,
> but we never get up till the sergeant brings our breakfast up to bed.
> Oh, oh, oh, it's a lovely war.
>
> What do we want with eggs and ham when we've got plum and apple jam?

> Form fours. Right turn. How shall we spend the
> money we earn?
> Oh, oh, oh, it's a lovely war.

Note that Joan Littlewood's memorable 1963 stage show about the First World War – which included this song among many others of the time – was actually entitled *Oh What a Lovely War* (i.e. 'what' for 'it's – and no exclamation marks). A specific credit for this title is still given to Ted Allan. When Richard Attenborough directed a film of the show (in 1969), the title acquired just one of the exclamation marks from the original song and became *Oh! What a Lovely War*.

oil slick
Could this phrase first have been used to describe what a crippled or destroyed submarine left behind, during the Second World War? No. The term was used in a non-military sense by 1887 and had, it would seem, already been used in the First World War: 'The submarine when running close beneath the surface leaves what is known as an "oil slick". That is, the oil that is discharged in the exhausts floats on the top of the water in tell-tale streaks ... "Oil Slick" is American terminology. The British Admiralty did not approve at first' – *The Saturday Evening Post* (12 October 1918).

Old Bill
Nickname for an old soldier or veteran, derived from a character created by the British cartoonist Bruce Bairnsfather (1888–1959) in the First World War. A bewhiskered, cheerful soldier, Old Bill became the

embodiment of the grumbling but irrepressible infantryman – particularly after the cartoon published first in *The Bystander* and then in *Fragments from France* (1915), depicting the gloomy soldier and a comrade, taking refuge in a shell-hole, with Bill saying: **'Well, if you knows of a better 'ole, go to it'** [this is the correct wording, though it is often rendered as 'If you know a better 'ole, go to it.'] The cartoon series, with its philosophical acceptance of one's lot, became enormously popular. A musical (London, 1917; New York, 1918) and two films (UK 1918; US 1926), based on the strip, all had the title *The Better 'Ole*. (The more modern use of the term for a policeman – later simply 'the Bill' – may have to do with the fact that many policemen in the 1920s/1930s wore the walrus moustache that the cartoon character sported.)

Old Blood 'n' Guts
Nickname of George S. Patton (1885–1945), US general and Commander of the Third Army in the Second World War. A brilliantly forceful soldier, who liked to be regarded as a 'tough guy' (he was flamboyant, and carried a pearl-handled revolver in an open holster); but he could be emotional and friendly – disliked by some, adored by others. The nickname is supposedly a tribute to his aggressive determination.

Old Contemptibles
Nickname gladly taken unto themselves by rank-and-file members of the British Expeditionary Force who crossed the English Channel in 1914 to join the French and Belgians against the German advance. It was alleged that Kaiser Wilhelm II had described the army as 'a contemptibly little

army' (referring to its *size* rather than its *quality*). The British press was then said to have mistranslated this so that it made him appear to have called them a 'contemptible little army'. Indeed, BEF Routine Orders for 24 September 1914 contained what was claimed to be a copy of orders issued by the German Emperor on 19 August: 'It is my Royal and Imperial command that you concentrate your energies for the immediate present upon one single purpose, and that is that you address all your skill and all the valour of my soldiers to exterminate first, the treacherous English [and] walk over General French's contemptible little army.'

The truth, as revealed by Arthur Ponsonby in *Falsehood in War-Time* (1928), is that the whole episode was a propaganda ploy masterminded by the British. The Kaiser's alleged words became widely known, but an investigation during 1925 in the German archives failed to produce any evidence of the order ever having been issued. The ex-Kaiser himself said: 'On the contrary, I continually emphasized the high value of the British Army, and often, indeed, in peace-time gave warning against underestimating it.' It is now accepted that the phrase was devised at the War Office by Sir Frederick Maurice.

Old Crock
Nickname of Anthony C. McAuliffe (1898–1975), US general in the Second World War. His nickname was self-inflicted in a talk to his men. See also NUTS!

Old soldiers never die, they simply fade away
Line from a British Army song of the First World War. It is a parody of the gospel hymn 'Kind Thoughts Can Never

Die'. J. Foley copyrighted a version of the parody in 1920. *Old Soldiers Never Die* was title of a First World War memoir by Frank Richards (creator of 'Billy Bunter'), published in 1933.

On les aura! [Let 'em have it!]
From a French Government poster of the First World War seeking war loans. This was revived in the Second World War, as also in the US, with the slogan, 'Let 'em have it. Buy Extra Bonds.'

One of our aircraft is missing
Phrase from Second World War news bulletins and, hence, the title of a feature film (UK 1941). In *A Life in Movies* (1986), Michael Powell writes: 'After I returned from Canada and I had time to listen to the nine o'clock news on the BBC, I had become fascinated by a phrase which occurred only too often: "One of our aircraft failed to return".' He determined to make a film about such a failed bombing mission. 'Our screenplay, which was half-finished, was entitled *One of Our Aircraft is Missing*. We were never too proud to take a tip from distributors, and we saw that the original title, *One of Our Aircraft Failed to Return*, although evocative and euphonious, was downbeat.' Eventually, Walt Disney came up with a film called *One of Our Dinosaurs is Missing* (US 1975).

Operation Sea-Lion
The code name for the German plan to invade the United Kingdom after the fall of France in the Second World War –

in German, *Seelöwe*. It was announced by Hitler in July 1940 and cancelled in October of that year. 'Our excellent Intelligence confirmed that the operation "Sea Lion" had been definitely ordered by Hitler' – Winston Churchill, *Their Finest Hour*, Chap. 14 (1949).

over the top

The expression 'to go over the top' originated in the trenches of the First World War by 1916. It was used to describe the method of charging over the parapet and out of the trenches on the attack. Partridge/*Long Trail* adds: 'The phrase was originally *over the top and the best of luck*, but as casualties increased and so many attacks ended in disaster, "and the best of luck" was either omitted or spoken in bitter irony.' Now meaning 'exaggerated in manner of performance; "too much" ' – in a curious transition, the phrase was later adopted for use by show-business people when describing a performance that had gone beyond the bounds of restraint, possibly to the point of embarrassment.

over there

'Over There' was the title of a song written by George M. Cohan on 6 April 1917 after reading a newspaper headline that the US had entered the First World War. It became America's major song of the First World War and Cohan received the Congressional Medal for having written it. It referred, of course, to France or the Western Front or to Europe as a whole:

Over there, over there,
Send the word, send the word, over there.
That the Yanks are coming, the Yanks are coming,
… And we won't come back till it's o-ver o-ver there.

As for 'over *here*':

overpaid, overfed, oversexed and over here
Phrase describing American troops in Britain during the
Second World War. Ascribed to Tommy Trinder, the
English comedian (1909–89) in *The Sunday Times* (4 January
1976). This was Trinder's own full-length version of a
popular British expression of the early 1940s. He certainly
did not invent it, although he may have done much to
popularize it. Partridge/*Catch Phrases* makes no mention of
Trinder and omits the 'overfed'. It was quoted in *The
Washington Post* (30 April 1944) as 'They're over-paid,
they're over-sexed, and they're over here.' As 'over-sexed,
over-paid and over here' it is also said to have been a popular
expression about American troops in Australia 1941–45 –
according to *The Dictionary of Australian Quotations* (1984).

Owing to the international situation
A catch-all phrase to explain why something is not
happening or has been cancelled, from the Second World
War. 'Owing to the international situation the match with
St. Trinian's has been postponed' – caption to Ronald Searle
cartoon in *Lilliput* magazine, IX. IV. (1941).

'Pack Up Your Troubles in Your Old Kit Bag'

Title of a popular song written by 'George Asaf' (George and Felix Powell) for a London show, *Her Soldier Boy* (1915). It goes on:

> … And smile, smile, smile.
> While you've a lucifer to light your fag,
> Smile, boys, that's the style.
> What's the use of worrying?
> It never was worth while,
> So, pack up your troubles in your old kit bag,
> And smile, smile, smile.

Panic stations!

Light-hearted use of the old British naval term 'be at panic stations', meaning 'to be prepared for the worst' (and current from the beginning of the Second World War). Nowadays, it may mean no more than 'Don't get in my way, I've got a crisis on!' 'Immediately after the explosion "Panic stations" was ordered, followed in due course by "Abandon ship"' – *The Times* (13 November 1918).

Panzer division

A German armoured unit in the Second World War, from *Panzer* meaning a tank or armoured car – from 1934 or earlier – and ultimately from the 12th-century Middle High German word for 'armour/coat of mail'.

Pathfinders

Specially trained bomber crews, their aircraft equipped with the latest navigational devices, who flew ahead of the main bombing force in the latter part of the Second World War to identify and light up the target. Formed in 1942 under the command of Air Commodore D.C.T. Bennett, formerly a station commander in No 4 Group of Bomber Command, the pioneer night bombing group. Inevitably, his nickname became 'Pathfinder' Bennett.

Peace for our time

On returning from signing the Munich agreement (30 September 1938), Prime Minister Neville Chamberlain spoke from a window at 10 Downing Street – 'Not of design but for the purpose of dispersing the huge multitude below' (according to his biographer Keith Feiling). He said, 'My good friends, this is the second time in our history that there has come back from Germany to Downing Street peace with honour. I believe it is peace for our time. Go home and get a nice quiet sleep.' Two days before, when someone had suggested the Disraeli phrase 'Peace with honour', Chamberlain had impatiently rejected it. Now, according to John Colville, *Footprints in Time* (1976), Chamberlain used the phrase at the urging of his wife.

Chamberlain's own phrase 'Peace for our time' is often misquoted as '**Peace in our time**' – as by Noël Coward in the title of his 1947 play set in an England conquered by the Germans. Perhaps Coward, and others, were influenced by the phrase from the Book of Common Prayer, 'Give peace in our time, O Lord'. The year before Munich,

Punch (24 November 1937) showed 'Peace in our time' as a wall slogan.

(A) period of great boredom interspersed with moments of great excitement

In Richard Hillary's *The Last Enemy* (1942), the RAF pilot refers to a quote about war to this effect. He may also have broadcast on the BBC a variation that described participating in the Battle of Britain as, rather, 'long boring hours interspersed with moments of tremendous exhilaration'. The saying probably pre-dates the Second World War. Subsequently applied to army life, another version is to be found in Spike Milligan's *Adolf Hitler: My Part in His Downfall* (1974) in which a Major talks of 'long periods of boredom broken by moments of great excitement.' In the BBC radio comedy *The Betty Witherspoon Show* (11 May 1974) there is a description of air transport as 'hours of boredom interrupted by moments of stark terror.'

phoney war

At first, when war was declared in September 1939, nothing happened. Neville Chamberlain talked of a 'Twilight War' and on 22 December Édouard Daladier, the French Prime Minister, said: '*C'est une drôle de guerre*' [It's a phoney war – spelt 'phony' in the US]. On 19 January 1940, the *News Chronicle* had a headline: 'This is Not a Phoney War: Paris Envoy.' And Paul Reynaud employed the phrase in a radio speech on 3 April 1940: ' "It must be finished", that is the constant theme heard since the beginning. And that means that there will not be any "phoney peace" after a war which is

by no means a "phoney war".' Though speaking French,
Reynaud used the phrase in English. Another, lesser-known,
term for this time is 'sitzkrieg' – compared with the *blitzkrieg*
that Hitler had been waging across the Channel (see BLITZ).

(It's a) piece of cake

Meaning that something is simple, no bother, and easily
achieved. Comparisons are inevitable with other food
phrases like 'easy as pie' and 'money for jam', but the general
assumption seems to be that it is a shortened form of 'It's as
easy as eating a piece of cake'. The earliest *OED* citation is
American and from 1936, though the phrase may not be of
actual US origin. It was especially popular in the RAF
during the Second World War, hence the appropriate title
Piece of Cake, applied by Derek Robinson to his novel (1983)
about RAF fliers in the Second World War, which was
turned into a TV mini-series in 1988. In 1943, C.H. Ward-
Jackson published *It's a Piece of Cake*.

pillbox

A small, box-like concrete building erected in great numbers
on all sides in the Second World War and built to resist
shellfire. Pillboxes were used as observation posts (for
example, against invasion) or for sheltering small guns.
Introduced in 1917 by the Germans in Flanders.

pocket battleship

A type of warship, small but powerful, that Germany built
after the First World War, supposedly keeping within the
limit of 10,000 tons as stipulated by the Treaty of Versailles.

pom pom (gun)

In the First World War, this was the name given to a type of heavy machine gun firing one-pound (0.5kg) shells and probably derived from the 'pom-pom-pom' sound it made when in action. In the Boer War, the name had been given to the Maxim gun. In the Second World War, it was the name given to rapid-firing anti-aircraft guns on ships.

POW

From the First World War onwards, this became a common abbreviation for 'prisoner of war'.

Praise the Lord and pass the ammunition!

Phrase of religious pragmatism. Said in 1941 – and subsequently used as the title of a song by Frank Loesser (1942) – the authorship of this saying is disputed. It may have been said by an American naval chaplain during the Japanese attack on Pearl Harbor. Lieut. Howell M. Forgy (1908–83) is one candidate. He was on board the US cruiser *New Orleans* on 7 December 1941 and encouraged those around him to keep up the barrage when under attack. His claim is supported by a report in *The New York Times* (1 November 1942). Another name mentioned is that of Captain W.H. Maguire. At first Captain Maguire did not recall having used the words but a year later said he might have done. Either way, the expression actually dates from the time of the American Civil War.

(The) price of petrol has been increased by one penny

' "The price of petrol has been increased by one penny" – Official' is the caption to a cartoon by Philip Zec published in the *Daily Mail* (6 March 1942). It showed a torpedoed sailor adrift on a raft and suggested that fuel companies were making a profit on the back of human lives. The caption was suggested by the journalist 'Cassandra' (William Connor) and led to the paper almost being suppressed by the Government.

pushing up the daisies

Dead and buried. The terms 'toes turned up to the daisies' and 'under the daisies' were current from the middle of the 19th century, but 'pushing up the daisies' seems to come from the First World War. Wilfred Owen's poem 'A Terre (Being the Philosophy of Many Soldiers)' (1917–18) has it:

> 'I shall be one with nature, herb, and stone.'
> Shelley would tell me. Shelley would be stunned;
> The dullest Tommy hugs that fancy now.
> 'Pushing up daisies' is their creed, you know.
> To grain, then, go my fat, to buds my sap,
> For all the usefulness there is in soap.

Put out that light!

Cry of the air-raid warden during the BLACKOUTS of the Second World War. Any breach of the regulations that no light should be seen escaping from house windows, from car headlamps or even from the tip of a cigarette could lead to an appearance in court and the possibility of a stiff fine. The cry was recalled like this in 'The Aftermyth of War' sketch of the revue *Beyond the Fringe* (1961), but an episode of *Dad's Army* (6 November 1970) was, rather, given the title, 'Put That Light Out!' This seems to have been an equally popular version.

quisling

A traitor and collaborator. The word was adopted into English from the name of Vidkun Quisling, a former Minister of Defence in Norway who formed a national union party and supported the invasion of his country by the Germans in 1940. He became Minister-President under the Nazi occupation and head of a puppet government. After the German defeat he was tried and shot in 1945. 'Comment in the Press urges that there should be unremitting vigilance also against possible "Quislings" inside the country [Sweden]' – *The Times* (15 April 1940).

race to the sea

This phrase dates from the autumn of 1914 and was used during the early months of the First World War. In his *English History 1914–45* (1966), A.J.P. Taylor writes: 'Both combatant lines hung in the air. Some 200 miles [322km] of open country separated the German and French armies from the sea. Each side tried to repeat the original German strategy of turning the enemy line. This was not so much a "race to the sea", its usual name, as a race to outflank the other side before the sea was reached. Both sides failed.' Martin Gilbert uses the phrase evocatively of a phase of the Second World War in the official biography of Winston Churchill, Vol. 6, Chap. 21 (1983): 'As dawn broke on May 26 [1940], the news from France dominated Churchill's thoughts, and those of his advisers and staff. The road to Dunkirk was open. The race to the sea was about to begin.' In his own *The Second World War*, Vol. 2, Churchill entitled the chapter dealing with Dunkirk 'The March to the Sea'.

radar

So familiar is this word now that it is worth remembering it has a down-to-earth derivation. It is made up of the first part of the word '*ra*dio' and the initial letters of '*d*etection *a*nd *r*anging'. The word was established – along with the invention – during the first two years of the Second World War. The device was the brainchild of Sir Robert Watson-Watt, who had developed it in 1933–5. It was first used in the Battle of Britain, though originally referred to as a 'radiolocator' or as 'RDF' [Radio Direction-Finding]. The actual word 'Radar' seems to have been suggested by two US Navy Lieutenant Commanders in 1940.

rationing

The official control of items such as fuel, food and clothing, as they became scarce during the Second World War. A coupon or stamp system allowing for such fair purchase was introduced in Britain in January 1940 and in the US in December 1941. The word had already been used, however, during the First World War and with reference to earlier Government controls – in, for example, the Siege of Paris.

Red Baron

Manfred Freiherr von Richthofen (1892–1918) was a German fighter pilot of the First World War, not only a hero to his own side but greatly respected by Allied airmen. He flew a red Fokker plane and led what became known as **Richthofen's Circus**, which created havoc. He was credited with destroying 80 planes. When shot down over Allied lines he was given a military funeral, with a bearer party of six captains and a firing party provided by the Australian Flying Corps.

Remember the — !

A common form of sloganeering, particularly as a way of starting conflicts or keeping them alive, especially in the US. From the two world wars, we have: **Remember Belgium!** –

originally a recruiting slogan of the First World War, referring to the invasion of Belgium by the Germans at its start. It eventually re-emerged with ironic emphasis amid the mud of Ypres, encouraging the rejoinder: 'As if I'm ever likely to forget the bloody place!' (Partridge/*Catch Phrases*). 'My mother used to say this to me in the 1930s when, as a small boy, I showed signs of being about to do something she disapproved of. The meaning was clear – "remember what happened to *them*" – presumably in 1914' – Guy Braithwaite, Middlesex (1998). Then came **Remember the Lusitania!**, which followed the sinking of that ship by the Germans in 1915. **Remember Pearl Harbor!** followed from the 1941 incident.

Remember there's a war on

See DON'T YOU KNOW THERE'S A WAR ON?

reparations

Originally this word meant 'reconciliation' but after the Treaty of Versailles it came to refer to the punitive charges made by the Allies on the Germans to compensate them for their losses in the First World War. A chapter heading of the *Treaty of Peace* (1920) is 'Reparation'.

Resistance

The network of small groups acting against the German occupiers in France during the Second World War was known as '*la Résistance*'. It was formed in June 1940 with the object of resisting the German occupying forces and the Vichy Government. Elsewhere in Europe, such groups tended to be referred to as 'the underground'. 'General de Gaulle broadcast from London a message to the French nation last night. The text of his speech is as follows … "Whatever happens the flame of French resistance must not and shall not be extinguished"' – *The Times* (19 June 1940).

Retreat? Hell, no! We just got here!
An attributed remark, made by US Captain Lloyd S. William when advised by the French to retreat, shortly after his arrival at the Western Front in the First World War. Or, specifically refers to the retreat from Belloar (5 June 1918). Untraced and unverified. Compare: 'Retreat, hell! We're just fighting in another direction' – attributed to General Oliver Prince Smith, US Marine Corps, at Changjin Reservoir, North Korea (autumn 1950).

Russians with snow on their boots
In September 1914, within a month of war being declared, there was an unfounded rumour that a million Russian troops had landed at Aberdeen in Scotland and passed through England on their way to the Western Front. The detail that they were seen to have had 'snow on their boots' was supposed to add credence to the report. This had to be officially denied by the War Office. Arnold Bennett was one of several people who noted the rumour at the time. In his *Journals* (for 31 August 1914), he wrote: 'The girls came home with a positive statement from the camp that 160,000 Russians were being landed in Britain, to be taken to France … The statement was so positive that at first I

almost believed it … In the end I dismissed it, and yet could not help hoping … The most curious embroidery on this rumour was from Mrs A.W., who told Mrs W. that the Russians were coming via us to France, where they would turn treacherous to France and join Germans in taking Paris … This rumour I think took the cake.'

In Osbert Sitwell's *Great Morning* (1951), he records how his 'unusually wise and cautious' 16-year-old brother Sacheverell had written to tell him: 'They saw the Russians pass through the station last night … and Miss Vasalt telephoned to Mother this afternoon and said trains in great number had passed through Grantham Station all day with the blinds down. So there must, I think, be some truth in it, don't you?'

In *Falsehood in War-Time* (1928), Arthur Ponsonby said of the phrase 'Russians with snow on their boots', that 'nothing illustrates better the credulity of the public mind in wartime and what favourable soil it becomes for the cultivation of falsehood'. Several suggestions have been made as to how this false information caught hold: that the Secret Service had intercepted a telegram to the effect that '100,000 Russians are on their way from Aberdeen to London' (without realizing that this referred to a consignment of Russian eggs); that a tall, bearded fellow had declared in a train that he came from 'Ross-shire', and so on. In fact, the British Ambassador to Russia *had* requested the dispatch of a complete army corps, but the request was never acceded to.

Ponsonby commented: 'As the rumour had undoubted military value, the authorities took no steps to deny it …

[but] an official War Office denial of the rumour was noted by the *Daily News* on September 16, 1914.' A *Punch* cartoon (23 September 1914) had the caption:

> *Porter:* 'Do I know if the Rooshuns has really come through England? Well, Sir, if this don't prove it, I don't know what do. A train went through here full, and when it come back I knowed there'd bin Rooshuns in it, 'cause the cushions and floors was covered with snow.'

san fairy ann
This expression, meaning 'it doesn't matter; why worry?',
dates from the First World War and is a corruption of the
French *ça ne fait rien* [that's nothing, it makes no odds, it
does not matter, don't worry].

saturation bombing
A raid of massed bombers on target areas rather than on a
specific target – in the Second World War, by 1942. It came
into use following the raid by 1,000 British bombers on
Cologne in May 1942, when 2,000 tons of bombs were
dropped in 90 minutes. The opposite is 'precision bombing',
also known by 1942–43.

(The) sea shall not have them
Motto of Coastal Command's Air-Sea Rescue Service during
the Second World War. In John Harris, *The Sea Shall Not
Have Them* (1953; film UK 1954), it is mentioned as, rather,
'the motto of Air-Sea Rescue High-Speed Launch Flotillas'.

Second Front now
An unofficial political slogan in the Second World War, dating
from 1942–43. This was a demand chalked on walls (and
supported by the Beaverbrook press) for an invasion of the
European mainland, particularly one in collaboration with the
Soviet Union. It followed Britain and Russia becoming co-
belligerents in 1941. Mostly Leftists wanted it. The Allied
military command disagreed and preferred to drive Axis

S

troops out of North Africa and the Mediterranean first. Churchill's argument against a Second Front was that Britain's resources were fully stretched already. He entitled a chapter in Vol. 4 of his *Second World War* 'SECOND FRONT NOW!' and implies that the 'First Front' was that between the Soviet Union and Germany in Russia. Indeed, he writes that the Russians 'had every right to call [this] the First Front'. In April 1942, the US proposed the first major offensive in alliance with Great Britain against the Germans. This 'Second Front' was to be an invasion in Western Europe and eventually resulted in the D-Day landings of June 1944.

set Europe ablaze

Instruction from Winston Churchill on the establishment of the Special Operations Executive to coordinate acts of subversion against enemies overseas. This ringing call was one of the last Churchillisms to become publicly known. E.H. Cookridge wrote in *Inside S.O.E.* (1966): 'The Special Operations Executive was born on 19 July 1940' on the basis of a memo from Churchill ' "to coordinate all action by way of subversion and sabotage against the enemy overseas". Or, as the Prime Minister later put it "to set Europe ablaze".' The title of the first chapter of Cookridge's book is 'Set Europe Ablaze'.

Set the people free

Slogan used by the Conservative Party which helped it regain power, with Winston Churchill as Prime Minister, in the 1951 General Election. The slogan was taken from the lyrics of a patriotic song of the Second World War. In 'Song of Liberty' (1940), A.P. Herbert put words to the *nobilmente* theme from Edward Elgar's *Pomp and Circumstance March No. 4*: 'All men must be free / March for liberty with me / Brutes and braggarts may have their little day, / We shall never bow the knee. / God is drawing His sword / We are marching with the Lord / Sing, then, brother, sing, giving ev'ry thing, / All you are and hope to be, / To set the peoples free.'

shell shock
A British term from the First World War to describe psychological disturbance in troops exposed to shellfire, by 1915. *IHAT* suggests that the Americans preferred the term **battle fatigue**.

shock troops
Name given to specially selected and trained forces taking part in assault operations against strongly defended positions of the enemy. From the First World War and apparently derived from the German *Stosstruppen*.

Sieg heil!
The typical verbal salute given by German troops in the Second World War, especially at Nazi rallies. *Sieg* means 'victory, conquest or triumph' and so *Sieg heil* means 'Hail victory!', though on occasions perhaps little more than 'Hurrah!' By 1940.

(awakening a) sleeping giant
After the Japanese attack on Pearl Harbor in December 1941, Isoroku Yamamoto, the admiral and commander-in-

S

chief who devised it, is supposed to have said: 'I fear we
have only awakened a sleeping giant, and his reaction will
be terrible.' This was so attributed by A.J.P. Taylor in *The
Listener* (9 September 1976) but, as the Library of
Congress's *Respectfully Quoted* makes clear, the only
suggestion that Yamamoto said any such thing is in the
screenplay of *Tora! Tora! Tora!* (US 1970), in which the
words are: 'I fear all we have done is to awaken a sleeping
giant and fill him with a terrible resolve.' However, the
month after Pearl Harbor, he *did* write in a letter: 'A military
man can scarcely pride himself on having "smitten a
sleeping enemy"; in fact, to have it pointed out is more a
matter of shame.' Yamamoto had studied and worked in the
US and earlier was opposed to Japanese participation in the
Second World War.

smoke screen

Literally what it says: a screen of smoke created so that
troops could advance undetected. A term from the First
World War, by 1915. 'The "smoke screen" – an accepted and
extensively practised ruse in naval strategy, and now
adopted by its mosquito colleagues of the air' – F.A. Talbot,
Aeroplanes (1915), suggesting an earlier provenance.

SNAFU

Acronym for 'Situation Normal All Fouled/Fucked Up', of
American origin, probably from the Services, by early in the
Second World War. 'An expression conveying the common
soldier's laconic acceptance of the disorder of war and the
ineptitude of his superiors' – *OED*.

soft underbelly

The phrase 'soft underbelly', for a vulnerable part, appears
to have originated with Winston Churchill. Speaking in the
House of Commons on 11 November 1942, he said: 'We
make this wide encircling movement in the Mediterranean
... having for its object the exposure of the under-belly of
the Axis, especially Italy, to heavy attack.' In his *The Second
World War*, Vol. 4 (1951), he describes a prior meeting with
Stalin in August 1942, at which he had outlined the same
plan: 'To illustrate my point I had meanwhile drawn a
picture of a crocodile, and explained to Stalin with the help
of this picture how it was our intention to attack the soft
belly of the crocodile as we attacked his hard snout.'
Somewhere, subsequently, the 'soft' and the 'underbelly'
must have joined together to produce the phrase in the form
in which it is now used.

soldier's farewell

An insulting farewell that takes various forms, e.g. 'Goodbye
and fuck you!' Known since before the First World War. By
the Second World War, a 'soldier's farewell' was also used to
describe maintenance payments payable by the father of an
illegitimate child ...

something wrong with our bloody ships today

What the English admiral Sir David Beatty (later 1st Earl
Beatty) (1871–1936) actually said was, 'There seems to be
something wrong with our bloody ships today, Chatfield.'
The Battle of Jutland on 31 May–1 June 1916 was the only
major sea battle of the First World War. It was, on the face

of it, an indecisive affair. The British grand fleet under its Commander-in-Chief, Sir John Jellicoe, failed to secure an outright victory. Admiral Beatty, commanding a battle-cruiser squadron, saw one ship after another sunk by the Germans. At 4.26 on the afternoon of 31 May, the *Queen Mary* was sunk with the loss of 1,266 officers and men. This was what led Beatty to make the above comment to his Flag Captain, Ernle Chatfield. Sometimes the words 'and with our system' have been added to the remark, as also 'Turn two points to port' (i.e. nearer the enemy) and 'Steer two points nearer the enemy', but Chatfield denied that anything more was said (source: *Oxford Dictionary of Quotations*, 1953 and 1979).

Ultimately, the battle marked the end of any German claim to have naval control of the North Sea and, in that light, was a British victory, but Jutland was a disappointment at the time and has been chewed over ever since as a controversial episode in British naval history.

somewhere in ———

This construction originated for security reasons in the First World War so as to avoid censorship in correspondence. For example: 'somewhere in France', as in *Punch* (21 April 1915) and as in a letter from J.B. Priestley to his father (27 September 1915). Its use came to be broadened to anywhere one could not, or one did not want to, be too precise about. On 24 August 1941, Winston Churchill broadcast a report on his meeting with President Roosevelt: 'Exactly where we met is secret, but I don't think I shall be indiscreet if I go so far as to say that it was "somewhere in the Atlantic".' There was a film *Somewhere in England* (1940) that begat a series of British regional comedies with titles like *Somewhere in Camp / on Leave / in Civvies* and *in Politics*.

Southern Front
The least familiar of the several Second World War fronts, this one stretched from Switzerland along the Italian frontier to Trieste.

Speak for England, Arthur!
Interjection in the House of Commons (2 September 1939). On the eve of war, Prime Minister Neville Chamberlain appeared in the Commons holding out the prospect of a further Munich-type peace conference and did not announce any ultimatum to Germany. When the acting Labour leader, Arthur Greenwood, rose to respond, a Conservative MP shouted, 'Speak for England, Arthur!' For many years, it was generally accepted that the MP was Leo S. Amery and, indeed, he wrote in *My Political Life* (Vol. 3, 1955): 'It was essential that someone should … voice the feelings of the House and of the whole country. Arthur Greenwood rose … I dreaded a purely partisan speech, and called out to him across the floor of the House, Speak for England.' (Note, no 'Arthur'.) By 30 October, James Agate was writing in his diary (published in *Ego 4*) about the anthology for the forces he had been busy compiling called *Speak for England*: 'Clemence Dane gave me the title; it is the phrase shouted in the House the other day when Arthur Greenwood got up to speak on the declaration of the war.'

S

However, writing up an account of the session in *his* diary, Harold Nicolson (whose usual habit was to make his record first thing the following morning) wrote: 'Bob Boothby cried out, "*You* speak for Britain".' Boothby confirmed that he had said this when shown the diary passage in 1964.

The explanation would seem to be that after Amery spoke, his cry was taken up not only by Boothby but by others on the Tory benches. From the Labour benches came cries of 'What about Britain?' and 'Speak for the working classes!' Interestingly, nobody claims to have said the exact words as popularly remembered. The intervention went unrecorded in *Hansard*.

(to) spread alarm and despondency

Meaning, 'to have a destabilizing effect, purposely or not'. The phrase goes back to the Army Act of 1879: 'Every person subject to military law who ... spreads reports calculated to create unnecessary alarm or despondency ... shall ... be liable to suffer penal servitude.' When a German invasion was thought to be imminent at the beginning of July 1940, Winston Churchill had issued an 'admonition' to 'His Majesty's servants in high places ... to report, or if necessary remove, any officers or officials who are found to be consciously exercising a disturbing or depressing influence, and whose talk is calculated to spread alarm and despondency'. Prosecutions for doing this did indeed follow. Also during the Second World War, Lieut. Col. Vladimir Peniakoff ran a small raiding and reconnaissance force on the British side, which became known as 'Popski's Private

Army'. In his book *Private Army* (1950), he wrote:
'A message came on the wireless for me. It said "Spread
alarm and despondency" … The date was, I think, May
18th, 1942.'

squeezed until the pips squeak

To squeeze something until the pips squeak means 'to
extract the most [usually, money] from anything or
anyone'. This expression was apparently coined by Sir Eric
Geddes, a Conservative politician, shortly after the end of
the First World War. On the question of reparations,
Geddes said in an election speech at Cambridge (10
December 1918): 'The Germans, if this Government is
returned, are going to pay every penny; they are going to be
squeezed as a lemon is squeezed – until the pips squeak. My
only doubt is not whether we can squeeze hard enough, but
whether there is enough juice.' The previous night, Geddes,
who had lately been First Lord of the Admiralty, said the
same thing in a slightly different way as part of what was
obviously a stump speech: 'I have personally no doubt we
will get everything out of her that you can squeeze out of
a lemon and a bit more … I will squeeze her until you can
hear the pips squeak … I would strip Germany as she has
stripped Belgium.'

Stalag

In the Second World War this was the German name for a
prisoner-of-war camp and was a shortened form of
Stammlager, literally 'main camp'. These places were
numbered rather than named, hence 'Stalag 17' (as in the

S

1953 film title). 'Stalag Luft', as in the title of the 1990s TV series, referred to a POW camp for airmen.

(to) star shell
To illuminate no man's land and enemy trenches by night using a shell that releases a shower of stars on bursting. Known by the 1870s – in time for the First World War.

Stick it, Jerry!
Catchphrase from a sketch, 'The Bloomsbury Burglars', which was being performed by 1906, involving Lew Lake, a Cockney comedian (1874–1939). Playing a burglar, Lake would say it to his companion when they were throwing missiles at policemen pursuing them. Hence, it became a phrase of encouragement and was especially popular during the First World War. But the 'Jerry' here addressed is not a German and that nickname came from elsewhere – see BOCHE/FRITZ/HUN/JERRY/KRAUT.

Storm clouds are gathering over Europe
See (THE) GATHERING STORM.

storm troopers
Originally, like SHOCK TROOPS [from the German *Sturmtruppen*], these were known by 1917. Better known after the First World War as members of the German Nazi party's *Sturmabteilung* ('storm/attack division') or *S.A.*, formed in 1921 to police meetings but also to break up opposition. By the 1930s, their activities had spread to violent attacks on Jews and others. Also known as the

Brownshirts – after their uniform – they became, from 1934, the principal instrument of physical training and of the political indoctrination of German men.

strategic bombing
A British term for the bombing of specific targets (like factories) in the Second World War – as opposed to the generalized bombing of cities that the Germans had indulged in during the early part of the war. The aim of it is to disrupt the economy and lower morale and, hence, is the opposite of SATURATION BOMBING. By 1941.

S.W.A.L.K. [Sealed with a loving kiss]
Lovers' acronym on envelopes, possibly dating from the days of military censorship of letters in the First World War. Partridge/*Long Trail* omits the 'loving' and has, rather, just 'S.W.A.K.' He adds, 'Actually it was the censoring officer who did the sealing.'

tank

Why is a heavily armed vehicle carrying a gun called a tank? 'Not because it resembles a water tank but because, when the prototypes were being built and tested by the British during the First World War, this secret code name was applied by Col. Sir Ernest Swinton. This is because the workers were told they were engaged upon making a new type of portable water tank for use in Mesopotamia' – *IHAT*. '"Tanks" is what these new machines are generally called, and the name has the evident official advantage of being quite undescriptive' – *The Times* (18 September 1916).

task force

'An armed force organized for a special operation under a unified command, hence … any group of persons organized for a special task' – *OED*. Known by 1941, possibly of American origin. A film called *Task Force* (US 1949) was a 'flag-waver' (according to *Halliwell's Film Guide*) portraying an admiral about to retire recalling his struggle to promote the cause of aircraft carriers. In the early 1970s (according to *Halliwell's Television Companion*), there was a BBC TV series 'rather clumsily' entitled *Softly, Softly: Task Force*. Then, in 1982, the Falkland Islands were liberated from the Argentinians by what was widely referred to as the British Task Force.

T

that's the stuff to give the troops

Welcoming remark as food is placed on the table or after consuming it. Partridge/*Slang* dates this from the First World War but defines it simply as 'That's the idea, that's what we want', i.e. not necessarily about food. There is an obvious allusion in P.G. Wodehouse, *Carry On, Jeeves*, 'The Spot of Art' (1930): 'Forgive me, old man, for asking you not to raise your voice. A hushed whisper is the stuff to give the troops.' *The Stuff To Give the Troops* was the title of a BBC radio series (1942) entertaining servicemen during the Second World War.

'There'll Always Be an England'

Title of a popular patriotic song (1939) with words by Hugh Charles and music by Ross Parker. Charles and Parker were also responsible for WE'LL MEET AGAIN, written in the same year. At the outbreak of war in September 1939, the song became a hit for Vera Lynn and 200,000 copies of the sheet music were sold. The lyrics of the song are unmemorable but the title phrase has endured. The song's verse – 'I give you a toast, ladies and gentlemen … / May this fair dear land we love so well / In dignity and freedom dwell' – is an almost direct quotation of the toast from Noël Coward's play *Cavalcade* (1931): 'That one day this country of ours, which we love so much, will find dignity and greatness and peace again.'

'There's a Long, Long Trail (A-Winding)'

Title of an American song of the First World War. It was written in 1915 by Stoddard King (words) and Alonzo 'Zo' Elliott (music). It was very popular with the American doughboys but may echo 'The Long Trail', which is the title

of the envoi to *Barrack-Room Ballads* (1892) by Rudyard
Kipling. Hence *The Long Trail*, the title of a book on First
World War songs and slang, by John Brophy and Eric
Partridge (1965). The chorus goes:

> There's a long, long trail a-winding
> Into the land of my dreams,
> Where the nightingales are singing
> And a white moon beams:
> There's a long, long night of waiting
> Until my dreams all come true;
> 'Till the day when I'll be going down
> That long, long trail with you.

They shall not pass [Ils ne passeront pas]

Slogan popularly supposed to have been coined by Henri
Philippe Pétain, French marshal and politician (1856–1951),
the man who defended Verdun with great tenacity in 1916.
He is said to have uttered it on 26 February that year.
However, the first official record of the expression appears
in the Order of the Day for 23 June 1916 from General
Robert Nivelle (1856–1924) to his troops at the height of
the battle. His words were '*Vous ne laisserez pas passer*' [You
will not let them pass]. Alternatively, Nivelle is supposed to
have said these words to General Castelnau on 23 January
1916. To add further to the mystery, the inscription on the
Verdun medal was '*On ne passe pas*'. One suspects that the
slogan was coined by Nivelle and used a number of times by
him but came to be associated with Pétain, the more famous
'Hero of Verdun'.

T

The slogan saw further service as '*No pasarán*' on the Republican side during the Spanish Civil War.

They sought the glory of their country, / they see the glory of God

This is very much the sort of thing you find on First World War memorials – indeed, a trip to the National Inventory of War Memorials' website, www.ukniwm.org.uk, produces some 16,000 sightings … Sometimes the second part is, ' … and found the glory of their God' and a 1945 newspaper notice has the version, 'He sought the glory of his country, he is seeing the glory of God.' It might seem to be another of those standard memorial phrases that were coined during the 1914–18 war and then made available from a central source, but John Buchan's book *Pilgrim's Way* (1940) suggests otherwise. He is writing about his brother William, who died just before the First World War: 'There is a tablet to his memory in the antechapel of Brasenose [College, Oxford] on which is inscribed a sentence in Latin and adapted from Walter Savage Landor – *Patriae quaesivit gloriam, videt Dei.*' In *Selections* from Landor's writings, there is a piece entitled 'The Fate of a Young Poet', in which he describes how a village clergyman had beseeched him to write an epitaph on the poet in question. 'Being no friend to stone-cutter's charges, I entered not into biography, but wrote these few words:

Joannes Wellerby
LITERARUM QUAESIVIT GLORIAM,
VIDET DEI.

So with a simple change from 'He sought the glory of letters' to 'the glory of his country', that was how the wartime epitaph came about. The transition from Latin to English may have had more to do with Buchan's sister, Anna, who wrote under the name 'O. Douglas'. The dedication of her 1917 novel *The Setons* is: 'To my mother in memory of her two sons. They sought the glory of their country, they see the glory of God.'

Third Reich
The name given to Hitler's ruling government in Germany before and during the Second World War – *Reich* meaning 'empire, republic'. The First Reich was the Holy Roman Empire that lasted from the 9th century to 1806, the Second Reich was the German Empire (1871–1919), and the Third Reich was established by Hindenburg in 1933. It lasted until 1945.

Third World War
See WORLD WAR III.

This is Funf speaking!
Catchphrase from the BBC radio show *ITMA* (1939–49). Spoken sideways into a glass tumbler, this phrase was 'the embodiment of the nation's spy neurosis', according to the show's producer, Francis Worsley.

The first time 'Funf' appeared (played by Jack Train) was in the second edition of the show on 26 September 1939, just after the outbreak of the Second World War. Initially, he said, 'Dees ees Foonf, your favourite shpy!' Train recalled that when Worsley was searching for a name for the spy, he overheard his six-year-old son, Roger, trying to count in German: '*Eins, zwei, drei, vier, fünf* – and that's where he always got stuck. For a while it became a craze to start phone conversations with the words.

This ... is ... London!

A greeting that became familiar to Americans listening to Edward R. Murrow's radio reports from London during the Second World War. It was a natural borrowing from BBC announcers who had been saying 'This is London calling' from the earliest days of station 2LO in the 1920s. One of them, Stuart Hibberd, entitled a book of his broadcasting diaries *This Is London* (1950).

This was their finest hour

An illustrious phrase, from the peroration of Winston Churchill's speech to the House of Commons (18 June 1940) – a month after he became Prime Minister: 'If we fail, then the whole world, including the United States, including all that we have known and cared for, will sink into the abyss of a new Dark Age made more sinister, and perhaps more protracted, by the lights of perverted science. Let us therefore brace ourselves to our duties, and so bear ourselves that, if the British Empire and its Commonwealth last for a thousand years, men will still say, This was their finest hour.'

The Finest Hours was the title of a documentary film (UK 1964) about Churchill's life.

Tittle-tattle lost the battle

See under WALLS HAVE EARS.

(as dim as a) Toc H lamp

Very dim (unintelligent). Dates from the First World War,
in which there was a Christian social centre for British
'other ranks' opened at Talbot House in Poperinghe,
Belgium, in 1915 and named after an officer who was killed
– G.W.L. Talbot, son of a Bishop of Winchester. 'Toc H' was
signalese for 'Talbot House'. The institute continued long
after the war under its founder, the Revd P.B. ('Tubby')
Clayton. An oil lamp was its symbol.

Today —, tomorrow —

Slogan format, as in 'Today Germany, tomorrow the world'
[*Heute gehört uns Deutschland – morgen die ganze Welt –*
literally, 'Today Germany belongs to us – tomorrow the
whole world']. This was a Nazi political slogan in Germany
by the mid-1930s. Although John Colville, *The Fringes of
Power* (Vol. 1, 1985) states that by 3 September 1939, Hitler
'had already ... proclaimed that "Today Germany is ours;
tomorrow the whole world"', an example of Hitler actually
saying it has yet to be found. However, in *Mein Kampf*
(1925), Hitler had written: 'If the German people, in their
historic development, had possessed tribal unity like other
nations, the German Reich today would be the master of the
entire world.' The concept can be glimpsed in embryo in the
slogan of the National Socialist Press in the Germany of the
early 1930s: '*Heute Presse der Nationalsozialisten, Morgen
Presse der Nation*' [Today the press of the Nazis, tomorrow

T

the nation's press]. As also in the chorus of a song in the Hitler Youth 'songbook': *'Wir werden weiter marschieren / Wenn alles in Scherben fällt / Denn heute gehört uns Deutschland / Und morgen die ganze Welt* – which may be roughly translated as: 'We shall keep marching on / Even if everything breaks into fragments, / For today Germany belongs to us / And tomorrow the whole world.' Another version replaces the second line with *'Wenn Scheiße vom Himmel fällt'* [When shit from Heaven falls]. Sir David Hunt recalled hearing the song in 1933 or possibly 1934. By the outbreak of the Second World War, the format was sufficiently well known, as John Osborne recalled in *A Better Class of Person* (1981), for an English school magazine to be declaring: 'Now soon it will be our turn to take a hand in the destinies of Empire. Today, scholars; tomorrow, the Empire.' In the film *Forty-Ninth Parallel* (UK 1941), Eric Portman as a German U-boat commander gets to say, 'Today, Europe … tomorrow the whole world!' Interestingly, the format does seem to have existed outside Germany in the 1930s. In 1932, William B. Pitkin (1878–1953), Professor of Journalism at Columbia University, New York, published a book called *Life Begins at Forty* in which he dealt with 'adult reorientation' at a time when the problems of extended life and leisure were beginning to be recognized: 'Life begins at forty. This is the revolutionary outcome of our new era … TODAY it is half a truth. TOMORROW it will be an axiom.'

Tokyo Rose
Name given by US servicemen to Iva Ikuko Toguri D'Aquino (1916–2006), whose voice broadcasting to them

on Japanese radio in the Second World War told them they were sacrificing home comforts in a futile fight against invincible forces. She was but one of maybe a dozen such propaganda broadcasters who were given the same nickname. In fact, she broadcast as 'Orphan Ann'. She was not charged with any crime after the war but, as she was American-born and attempted to return to the US, she did eventually face charges of treason in 1949. She was found guilty on one count and was eventually given a Presidential pardon in 1977.

Tomorrow belongs to us/to me

Political *quasi*-slogan, chiefly remembered from the musical *Cabaret* (1968, film US 1972) in which Fred Ebb (words) and John Kander (music) wrote a convincing pastiche of a Hitler Youth song: 'The babe in his cradle is closing his eyes, the blossom embraces the bee, / But soon says a whisper, "Arise, arise", Tomorrow belongs to me. / O Fatherland, Fatherland, show us the sign your children have waited to see, / The morning will come when the world is mine, Tomorrow belongs to me.' The idea definitely seems to have been current in Nazi Germany. A popular song, *'Jawohl, mein Herr'*, featured in the 1943 episode of the German film chronicle *Heimat* (1984), includes the line, 'For from today, the world belongs to us.'

Tommy

Although this name for a British – but primarily English – soldier was established by 1893, it is so much associated with the First World War that its origins should be

T

mentioned here. This was short for 'Tommy Atkins', which became the generic name for such a soldier when, in 1815, the War Office issued the first 'Soldier's Account Book', which every soldier was provided with. The specimen form sent out with the book to show how details should be filled in bore at the place where a man's signature was required the hypothetical name 'Thomas Atkins'. This name continued to appear in later editions of the Soldier's Account Book until comparatively recent times. The term was made popular by Rudyard Kipling in his *Barrack Room Ballads* (1892).

Tora-tora-tora

Mitsuo Fuchida (1902–76) was leader of the Japanese attack on the US Pacific Fleet at Pearl Harbor (7 December 1941). On confirming that the fleet was indeed being taken by surprise at dawn, he uttered this codeword to signal that the rest of the attack plan could be put into operation. 'Tora' means 'tiger' – source: Gordon W. Prange, *At Dawn We Slept*, Chap. 61 (1982). Hence, *Tora! Tora! Tora!*, title of a film (US 1970) about the events leading up to Pearl Harbor.

trench warfare

At the beginning of the First World War, the Western Front was not fixed, with the Germans attacking France and Luxembourg and capturing most of the Belgian channel ports in the RACE TO THE SEA. Then in early 1915 Sir John French ordered the BEF to entrench. The Germans did likewise, beginning the bloody, gruelling three years of war in the trenches.

T.T.F.N. [Ta-ta for now]

Catchphrase from the BBC radio show *ITMA* (1939–49).
It was the farewell cry of 'Mrs Mopp' (Dorothy Summers)
after having presented her weekly gift to 'the Mayor'
(Tommy Handley). The character made her first appearance
in October 1941. It is said that during the Second World
War, quite a few people died with the catchphrase on their
lips. It would appear that *ITMA* coined the initialized form
of the farewell cry: it is recorded in its full form by 1883.

two minutes' silence

This observance was first carried out in both Britain and
the US on the first ARMISTICE DAY (11 November 1919).
Since 1946 it has been incorporated as part of Remembrance
Sunday commemorations. Subsequently the practice has
been copied to commemorate the dead in all kinds of
disasters and mishaps. 'The Great Silence ... At 11 o'clock
yesterday morning the nation, in response to the King's
invitation, paid homage to the Glorious Dead by keeping
a two minutes' silence for prayer and remembrance' – *The
Times* (12 November 1919).

U-boat

Name for a German submarine – short for *Unterseeboot*
[underseas boat] since the 1890s. Although such vessels
had featured in the American Civil War, the First World
War saw their first major deployment. Outside Germany,
'submarine' was shortened to **'sub'** in 1914.

umpity-poo

Partridge/*Slang* dates this 'nonsense word meaning "just a
little more"' to 1915–18 and derives it from the French *un
petit peu* [a small amount], a phrase presumably picked up
by British troops when in northern France. It seems it was
once considered as the title for Harry Watt's 1943 (army)
feature film – eventually entitled *Nine Men*. But this was
based on a story by Gerald Kersh, entitled 'Umpity Poo'.

unconditional surrender

In almost every conflict a time arrives when one of the
combatants decides that it will not be enough for the other
side to stop fighting: there will have to be 'unconditional
surrender'. The term had been used in the American Civil
War (by Ulysses S. Grant), but then, prior to the Armistice
in the First World War, the US General Pershing, in defiance
of President Wilson, had proposed to fight on until the
Germans agreed to 'unconditional surrender', i.e. that there
should be no separate peace agreements made. Later, at the
Casablanca conference of January 1943, President F.D.
Roosevelt produced his terms for ending the Second World

U

War, including the 'unconditional surrender' of Germany and Italy, a phrase he had used to his military advisers before leaving Washington and which was endorsed by Churchill (though the British would have preferred to exclude Italy). It was a controversial policy and later blamed for prolonging the war. According to Churchill's own account in Vol. 4 of *The Second World War*, Roosevelt admitted he had consciously been echoing Ulysses S. Grant, though the phrase had been used even before Grant in both the US and UK.

United Nations

This term was first hinted at in the 1941 Atlantic Charter signed by Churchill and Roosevelt before the US entered the war. It called for a permanent post-war system of general security. Roosevelt is said to have coined the name during Churchill's December 1941 visit to Washington. In January 1942, Churchill quoted to Roosevelt Byron's line, 'Here, where the sword united nations drew' from *Childe Harold's Pilgrimage*, when both agreed to substitute the term 'United Nations' for 'Associated Powers'. The name was first officially used on 2 January 1942 when 26 Allied nations pledged to continue the war effort jointly and not make any separate peace agreements.

(the tomb of the) Unknown Warrior

The idea of such a warrior's burial first came to a chaplain at the Front in 1916 after he had seen a grave in a back garden in Armentières, at the head of which was a rough wooden cross and the pencilled words, 'An unknown British Soldier'. At the conclusion of the war, a corpse for actual burial was selected from six such by a blindfolded British officer 'of very high rank'. The main inscription on what came to be known as the 'Unknown Warrior', buried in Westminster Abbey on Armistice Day 1920, is:

BENEATH THIS STONE RESTS THE BODY
OF A BRITISH WARRIOR
UNKNOWN BY NAME OR RANK
BROUGHT FROM FRANCE TO LIE AMONG
THE MOST ILLUSTRIOUS OF THE LAND
AND BURIED HERE ON ARMISTICE DAY
11 NOV: 1920, IN THE PRESENCE OF
HIS MAJESTY KING GEORGE V
HIS MINISTERS OF STATE
THE CHIEFS OF HIS FORCES
AND A VAST CONCOURSE OF THE NATION.

THUS ARE COMMEMORATED THE MANY
MULTITUDES WHO DURING THE GREAT
WAR OF 1914–1918 GAVE THE MOST THAT
MAN CAN GIVE LIFE ITSELF
FOR GOD
FOR KING AND COUNTRY
FOR LOVED ONES HOME AND EMPIRE
FOR THE SACRED CAUSE OF JUSTICE AND
THE FREEDOM OF THE WORLD.

THEY BURIED HIM AMONG THE KINGS BECAUSE HE
HAD DONE GOOD TOWARD GOD AND TOWARD
HIS HOUSE.

U

The inscription, which was written by Dean Ryle, includes the words, 'They buried him among the kings because he had done good toward God and toward his house.' This is based on 2 Chronicles 24:16 (concerning Jehoida, a 130-year-old man): 'And they buried him in the city of David among the kings, because he had done good in Israel, both toward God, and toward his house.' The line had earlier been used in the Abbey on the tomb of John de Waltham, Bishop of Salisbury, in 1395. He was buried in the Chapel of the Kings at Richard II's behest and to general indignation.

The American **'Unknown Soldier'** was buried on 11 November 1921 at Arlington National Cemetery, Virginia, and lies under the inscription:

> HERE RESTS IN
> HONORED GLORY
> AN AMERICAN
> SOLDIER
> KNOWN BUT TO GOD.

This form was also used on the graves of other unidentified soldiers in other American military cemeteries (such as the one at Brookwood, Surrey).

Subsequently, the Unknown at Arlington has been joined by three others whose graves are marked only by the dates of the wars in which they fell – '1941–1945' (The Second World War), '1950–1953' (Korea) and '1958–1975' (Vietnam). Collectively, the site is known as 'The Tomb of the Unknowns'.

There were, of course, many, many unidentified dead in the First World War and a standard epitaph was put on their gravestones, usually **'A Soldier of the Great War Known unto God.'** This was chosen by Rudyard Kipling, literary adviser to the Imperial War Graves Commission. In the majority of cases, the phrase was somehow abbreviated – as on a gravestone in the churchyard of St Peter and St Paul's, Aldeburgh:

A SEAMAN
OF THE GREAT WAR
ROYAL NAVY
7TH NOVEMBER 1914

(to go) up the line

In the First World War, this meant 'to travel from the base camps [in France] the twenty or thirty miles to within marching distance of the trenches, from billets in back areas to Front, support or reserve trenches' – Partridge/*Long Trail*. By 1916.

V-Day
See below.

'V' for victory

'Victory' came to be a watchword for the Second World War, just as 'Liberty' had been the one, for example, in the American Revolutionary War. The ' "V" for victory' slogan started as a piece of officially encouraged graffiti inscribed on walls in occupied Belgium by members of the anti-German 'freedom movement'. The Flemish word for freedom begins with a 'V' – *vrijheid* – and the French word for victory is, of course, *victoire*. The idea came from Victor de Laveleye, the BBC's Belgian Programme Organizer, who, in a broadcast on 14 January 1941, suggested that listeners should adopt the letter 'V' as 'a symbol of their belief in the ultimate victory of the Allies'. They were to go out and chalk it up wherever they could. From Belgium, the idea spread into the Netherlands and France and 'multitudes' of little Vs started appearing on walls in those countries.

Winston Churchill spoke of the **V-sign** as a symbol of 'the unconquerable will of the people of the occupied territories'. The symbol was expressed in other ways, too. The opening three notes of Beethoven's Fifth Symphony corresponded to the '... –' of the 'V' in Morse Code and, accordingly, the music was used in BBC broadcasts to occupied Europe. People gave the ' "V" for victory' salute with parted middle index fingers – though Winston Churchill confused matters by presenting his fingers the

V

wrong way round in a manner akin to the traditionally obscene gesture. Churchill's Private Secretary, John Colville, noted in his diary on 26 September 1941: 'The PM *will* give the V-sign with two fingers in spite of the representations repeatedly made to him that this gesture has quite another significance'.

After D-DAY, people started looking forward to **V-Day**, the day on which the war would end. When it came, the term **VE Day** (Victory in Europe Day) was used to mark the end of the war in Europe (8 May 1945) and **VJ Day** (Victory in Japan Day) to mark the end of the war with Japan (15 August 1945).

V-sign
See above.

Very well, alone
Caption to a cartoon in the London *Evening Standard* (18 June 1940) reflecting the mood of the British nation following the fall of France. The cartoon showed a British soldier confronting a hostile sea and a sky full of bombers. It was drawn by David Low, the British political cartoonist (1891–1963).

Victory at all costs
A rallying cry – though never, I think, used as an actual slogan – on the British side in the Second World War. It derives from the peroration of Winston Churchill's great speech on becoming Prime Minister (13 May 1940): 'You ask, what is our aim? I can answer in one word: victory,

victory at all costs, victory in spite of all terror, victory, however long and hard the road may be.'

Vinegar Joe

Nickname of US General Joseph Stilwell (1883–1946) – because of the acidity with which he expressed his opinions. During the Second World War, he was recalled from his command of Chinese and American troops in China-Burma-India after his tongue-lashing caused trouble with the Chinese Nationalist leader, Chiang Kai-Shek, in 1944. Also known as 'Old Turkey Neck' because of his unusually sunburned face and neck when in Burma.

walking wounded

In the First World War, those whose injuries were not so bad and who were still capable of walking. Probable origin was during the American Civil War. If the injuries were worse, then the troops were probably **stretcher cases** or, worse, BASKET CASES.

Walls have ears

A Government security slogan during the Second World War. The idea of inanimate objects being able to hear is, however, a very old one. In Vitzentzos Kornaros's epic poem *Erotokritos* (*c*.1645), there is the following couplet (here translated from the Greek):

> For the halls of our masters have ears and hear,
> And the walls of the palace have eyes and watch.

Jonathan Swift wrote in 1727, 'Walls have tongues, and hedges ears'.

From W.S. Gilbert's *Rosenkrantz and Guildenstern* (1891): 'We know that walls have ears. I gave them tongues / And they were eloquent with promises.' A French First World War poster is reported to have said: '*Taisez-vous! Méfiez-vous! Les oreilles ennemies vous écoutent* [Be silent! Be suspicious! Enemy ears are listening].'

Also, from the Second World War: **Tittle tattle lost the battle** and **Keep it under your hat** (US: **Keep it under your Stetson**). **Loose talk costs lives** and **Idle gossip**

sinks ships were additional US versions of the same theme, together with **The slip of a lip may sink a ship**; **Bits of careless talk are pieced together by the enemy**, and **Enemy ears are listening** (also US – used on posters from the Office of War Information).

The only drawback to these generally clever slogans was that they tended to reinforce the notion that there *were* spies and fifth columnists under every bed even if there were not.

war criminal
The issue of war crimes was raised (for the first time) at the Potsdam Conference in July/August 1945, though the concept had been around since 1906 at least. Churchill, Stalin and Truman believed that the Axis war criminals must be punished for their crimes. This led to the conducting of the Nuremberg Trials of November 1945 (and also of similar trials in Tokyo).

war effort
The effort a nation makes to win a war, or what a group of individuals does to that end. From the First World War. '(Heading) Britain's wonderful war effort' – *Maclean's Magazine* (January 1919).

war guilt
In the Treaty of Versailles (1919), there was a war-guilt clause blaming the Germans for the war and calling for the establishment of a League of Nations to settle international disputes.

War is too serious a business to be left to the generals
*[La guerre, c'est une chose trop grave pour la confier
à des militaires]*
In France, Parliament had suspended its sittings at the
outbreak of the First World War and the conduct of the war
had been entrusted to the Government and the General
Staff. By 1915, however, opinion was changing. It may have
been about this time that Clemenceau, who became French
Prime Minister again in 1917, uttered this, his most famous
remark. It was, apparently, quoted by Aristide Briand to
David Lloyd George: 'D. was very much taken with a
remark of Briand's to the effect that "this war is too
important to be left to military men". It is exactly D.'s view,
but unfortunately he never thought of putting it quite in
that way. I like D. to be the person to put things in a
particular clever way. Briand, however, seems to have the
knack' – *Lloyd George: A Diary by Frances Stevenson*, ed. A.J.P.
Taylor (1971), entry for 23 October 1916.

war plane
There had been no planes for military purposes before the
First World War and so this was the occasion for the
coinage. However: 'No one has any very definite ideas of
what the future type of war-plane will be like' – *Flight*
(16 December 1911).

(The) war to end wars
H.G. Wells had popularized this notion in a book he brought
out in 1914 with the title *The War That Will End War*. It was
not an original cry, having been raised in other wars, but by

the end of the First World War it was popularly rendered as 'the war to end wars'. On the afternoon of 11 November 1918, David Lloyd George announced the terms of the Armistice to the House of Commons and concluded: 'I hope we may say that thus, this fateful morning, came to an end all wars.' Later, Wells commented ruefully: 'I launched the phrase "the war to end war" and that was not the least of my crimes' – quoted in Geoffrey West, *H.G. Wells* (1930).

Sometimes it is said – for example, in *The Observer* Magazine (2 May 1993) – that it was a phrase of the 1930s and that there is no evidence the words were used at the time of the First World War. Clearly not the case.

(The) war to make the world safe for democracy

President Woodrow Wilson made a speech to Congress (2 April 1917), asking for a declaration of war against Germany. He said: 'The world must be made safe for democracy. Its peace must be planted upon trusted foundations of political liberty.' These words might never have been remembered had not Senator John Sharp Williams of Mississippi started clapping and continued until everyone joined in. In 1937, James Harvey Robinson commented: 'With supreme irony, the war to "Make the world safe for democracy" ended by leaving democracy more unsafe in the world than at any time since the collapse of the revolutions of 1848.'

(The) war's over, you know

Said to someone who is being noticeably and unnecessarily careful about not wasting food, electricity, etc. Current since the Second World War and a natural replacement for DON'T YOU KNOW THERE'S A WAR ON?

We have ways (and means) of making you talk

The threat by evil inquisitor to victim appears to have come originally from 1930s Hollywood villains and was then handed on to Nazi characters in fiction from the Second World War onwards. In the film *The Lives of a Bengal Lancer* (US 1934), Douglass Dumbrille, as the evil 'Mohammed Khan', says, 'We have ways to make men talk.' He means by forcing slivers of wood under the fingernails and setting fire to them … A typical 'film Nazi' use can be found in *Odette* (UK 1950), in which the eponymous French Resistance worker (Anna Neagle) is threatened with unmentioned nastiness by one of her captors. Says he: 'We have ways and means of making you talk.' Then, after a little stoking of the fire with a poker, he urges her on with: 'We have ways and means of making a woman talk.' Later, used in caricature, the phrase saw further action in programmes like the BBC radio show *Round the Horne* (e.g. 18 April 1965) and US TV *Laugh-In* (*circa* 1968) – invariably pronounced with a German accent.

Wehrmacht

The name used for the German armed forces between 1921 and 1945. The German literally means 'defence force'.

'We'll Meet Again'

The most evocative and stirring of Second World War songs – sung movingly and with a catch in the throat by Vera Lynn – was written in 1939 just in time to catch on as a stirring anthem, particularly for those separated from their loved ones by service in the armed forces. The words and music were by Ross Parker and Hughie Charles (who also helped write THERE'LL ALWAYS BE AN ENGLAND). The chorus goes:

> We'll meet again,
> Don't know where,
> Don't know when
> But I know we'll meet again some sunny day.

We never closed
A slogan coined by Vivien Van Damm, proprietor of the Windmill Theatre, London – a venerable comedy and strip venue – that was the only West End showplace to remain open during the Blitz in the Second World War. An obvious variant: 'We never clothed.'

Went the day well?
For a long time, the origin of this phrase was wrapped in mystery. 'Went the day well? / We died and never knew. / But, well or ill, / Freedom, we died for you' appears as the anonymous epigraph on screen at the start of a 1942 British film, *Went the Day Well?* (retitled *48 Hours* in the US). At the time the film was released, some thought it was a version of a Greek epitaph. Based on a story by Graham Greene entitled *The Lieutenant Died Last*, the film tells of a typical English village managing to repel Nazi invaders. The epigraph thus presumably refers to the villagers who die defending 'Bramley End'. Penelope Houston, in her 1992 British Film Institute monograph on the film, describes it as

a quotation from an anonymous poem that appeared in an anthology of tributes to people killed in the war to which Michael Balcon, head of Ealing Studios, contributed a memoir of the dead director Pen Tennyson. In fact, it was written by the English poet and academic J.M. Edmonds (1875–1958) and in its original form – 'Went the day well? we died and never knew; / But well or ill, England, we died for you' – was entitled 'On Some who died early in the Day of Battle' and appeared in 'Four Epitaphs', published in *The Times* (6 February 1918). It is said that it was based on a suggestion given Edmonds by Sir Arthur Quiller-Couch, who in turn got it from a Romanian folksong – *Notes & Queries* (Vol. 100). See also FOR YOUR TOMORROW WE GAVE OUR TODAY.

Western Front
The name given to the Front in Belgium and northern France in both World Wars. However, the principal use of the term, beginning in late 1914, was for the 600-mile (966km) stretch from Switzerland to the English Channel, and especially during the trench warfare that began in 1915. Hence, ALL QUIET ON THE WESTERN FRONT. The Germans called their line the Siegfried Line (see HANG OUT YOUR WASHING …).

(Daddy,) what did YOU do in the Great War?
An army recruitment slogan dating from about 1916. It appeared at the bottom of a poster showing an understandably appalled-looking family man puzzling over what to reply to the daughter on his knee who has obviously just asked him the question. This became a catchphrase in the form 'What did you do in the Great War, Daddy?' and gave rise to such

responses as 'Shut up, you little bastard. Get the Bluebell and go and clean my medals' – Partridge/*Catch Phrases*.

What price glory?

This phrase became firmly established in the language following its use as the title of a play about the stupidity of war by Laurence Stallings and Maxwell Anderson (1924; film US 1952). *What Price Glory?* further popularized the 'What price — ?' format phrase, questioning the sacrifices and compromises that may have to be made in order to carry out any sort of mission – which had been around since 1893, at least.

'(The) White Cliffs of Dover'

Title of song (1941) with words by Nat Burton and music by Walter Kent – who were both American, although this morale-building song, famously recorded by Vera Lynn, assumed almost the status of a national anthem in the Second World War. The white cliffs of Dover had long been deemed a symbol of Britain – not least in facing off invasion from Continental Europe. The song begins:

> There'll be blue birds over
> The white cliffs of Dover,
> Tomorrow
> Just you wait and see.
> There'll be joy and laughter
> And peace ever after,
> Tomorrow
> When the world is free.

whizzbang [or whizz-bang or whizbang]
The shell of a small-calibre, high-velocity German gun, so called from the noise it made. By 1915. Hence, the anonymous song popular in the First World War trenches, 'Hush, Here Comes a Whizzbang':

> Hush, here comes a whizzbang,
> Hush, here comes a whizzbang,
> Now, you soldier men, get down those stairs,
> Down in your dugouts and say your prayers.
> Hush, here comes a whizzbang,
> And it's making straight for you,
> And you'll see all the wonders of no-man's-land,
> If a whizzbang hits you.

This was a parody of the song 'Hush, Here Comes the Dream Man' by Robert Patrick Weston, Fred J. Barnes and Maurice Scott (written by 1911).

Who's absent? Is it you?
Recruitment slogan during the First World War. The posters also featured a picture of John Bull.

Women Of Britain Say – 'GO!'
Recruitment slogan featured on posters during the First World War.

Woodbine Willie
Nickname of the Revd. Geoffrey Studdert Kennedy, an English clergyman and poet (1883–1929). Kennedy was

known as 'Woodbine Willie' to troops in the First World War, because of his habit of walking through the trenches or casualty stations with a haversack full of Woodbine cigarettes. As an ordained minister, he was enrolled as Forces' chaplain in 1916 and served until 1919.

World War III/Third World War

And who was the first to raise the prospect and use either of these versions? A candidate is Tom Lehrer on the record album *That Was the Year That Was* (1965). His spoken introduction to the song 'So Long, Mom' goes: 'This year we've been celebrating the hundredth anniversary of the Civil War and the fiftieth anniversary of the beginning of World War I and the twentieth anniversary of the end of World War II – so all in all it's been a good year for the war buffs and a number of LPs and television specials have come out capitalizing on all this "nostalgia" with particular emphasis on the songs of the various wars. I feel that if any songs are going to come out of World War III we'd better start writing them now. I have one here. You might call it a bit of pre-nostalgia. This is the song that some of the boys sang as they went bravely off to World War III.'

As for the 'English' version, a very early contender – if not the actual first to use it – is Winston Churchill. In a speech to the House of Commons (20 August 1940) – and note the earliness of the date – he warned against 'elaborate speculations about the future shape which should be given to Europe or the new securities which must be arranged to spare mankind the miseries of a third World War …'

Wot no — ?

Informal protest slogan format from the early 1940s. The most common graffito of the second half of the 20th century in Britain – apart from 'Kilroy was here' (with which it was sometimes combined) – was the figure of 'Chad', 'Mr Chad' or sometimes 'The Chad'. He made his first appearances in the early stages of the Second World War, accompanied by protests about shortages of the time, such as, 'Wot no cake?', 'Wot no char?', 'Wot no beer?' 'Chad is the Watcher ... He peers over walls and asks, "Wot, no ...?"' – *Sunday Express* (2 December 1945).

Yesterday the trenches, today the unemployed
Unofficial political slogan current in 1923. This cry was heard in the aftermath of the First World War and prior to the first Labour election victory, under Ramsay MacDonald.

You can always take one with you
This informal slogan was suggested by Winston Churchill when invasion by the Germans was threatened in 1940. It was recalled by him in *The Second World War*, Vol. 2 (1949).

Your Britain – fight for it now
A Second World War slogan used on a poster showing an idyllic rural scene of hills, sheep and a shepherd.

Your country needs you!
The most famous recruiting slogan of all – inseparably linked to the picture of a mustachioed Field Marshal Lord Kitchener, with staring eyes and pointing finger – and presented as though a quotation from him, in capital letters, and with the 'YOU' extra large. Another version of the poster, also with a picture of Kitchener, announced: 'Britons, [Kitchener] wants you.' Kitchener was appointed Secretary of State for War on 6 August 1914, two days after the outbreak of what was to become known as 'the Great War'. He set to work immediately, intent on raising the 'New Armies' required to supplement the small standing army of the day, which he rightly saw would be inadequate for a major conflict. The poster was taken up by the

Parliamentary Recruiting Committee and first issued on
14 September the same year.

In fact, work on advertising for recruits had started the
year before, with some success. Then, towards the end of
July 1914, Eric Field of the tiny Caxton Advertising Agency
(owned by Sir Hedley Le Bas) received a call from a Colonel
Strachey, who 'swore me to secrecy, told me that war was
imminent and that the moment it broke out we should have
to start advertising at once'. That night, Field wrote an
advertisement headed **'Your King and Country Need You'**,
with the royal coat of arms as the only illustration. The day
after war was declared, 5 August, this appeared prominently
in the *Daily Mail* and other papers. The alliterative linking
of 'king' and 'country' was traditional. Francis Bacon (1625)
had written: 'Be so true to thyself, as thou be not false to
others; specially to thy King, and Country.' In 1913, J.M.
Barrie had included in his play *Quality Street*: 'If ... death
or glory was the call, you would take the shilling, ma'am ...
For King and Country.'

The appeal appeared in various forms but Kitchener
preferred these first slogans and insisted on finishing every
advertisement with 'God Save The King'. The drawing was
by the humorous artist Alfred Leete and the original is now
in the Imperial War Museum. (Margot Asquith's daughter
commented: 'If Kitchener was not a great man, he was, at
least, a great poster.')

The idea was widely imitated abroad. In the US, James
Montgomery Flagg's poster of a pointing Uncle Sam bore
the legend **'I Want You for U.S. Army'**. There was also a
version by Howard Chandler Christy featuring a woman

with a mildly come-hither look saying, **'I Want You for the Navy'**.

Your *courage*, your *cheerfulness*, your *resolution will bring us victory*

A Government morale-building slogan dating from 1939. One of the first posters after the outbreak of war, printed in vivid red and white, this caused a bitter outcry from those who resented any implication of 'Them and Us'. The slogan was suggested by A.P. Waterfield, a career civil servant at the Ministry of Information. He wanted 'A rallying war-cry that will … put us in an offensive mood at once' (quoted in *McLaine*). But it was judged to have fallen well short of the necessary belligerent tone. *The Times* thundered: 'The insipid and patronising invocations to which the passer-by is now being treated have a power of exasperation which is all their own. There may be no intrinsic harm in their faint, academic piety, but the implication that the public morale needs this kind of support, or, if it did, that this is the kind of support it would need, is calculated to promote a response which is neither academic nor pious.'

Your king and country need you

See YOUR COUNTRY NEEDS YOU.

zeppelin

Type of airship, named after Count Ferdinand von Zeppelin (1838–1917), the German aeronautical pioneer who designed and built them in about 1900. Sometimes referred to as a 'rigid DIRIGIBLE' because the gas bag was supported by a rigid frame 'and not just by internal gas pressure'. Zeppelins were used to bomb London and elsewhere during the First World War.

zero hour

The exact time a military operation is due to begin. Mostly British use in preference to the American H-Hour (see D-DAY). By 1917.

INDEX